THREADS OF DESTINY

By
J. P. Mercer

Threads of Destiny
A BookEnds Press Publication
PO Box 14513
Gainesville, Florida 32604
1-800-881-3208

Cover design by Sheri

For distribution information:

StarCrossed Productions, Inc.
PO Box 357474
Gainesville, Florida 32635-7474
www.starcrossedproductions.com

By The Author

Incommunicado (with Nancy Hill)

Dedication

This book is dedicated to Sue and her mother, Eileen.
Eileen
Born November 28, 1921
Resides now in Heaven.

The day you were born your blue eyes twinkled with the mischief of only the Irish, and I knew I had my hands full. Through the years your eyes shone with the love in your heart, my daughter, my friend. You stood beside me through the seasons of my life, loyal, steadfast, and devoted. My body was frail, my speech only heard as my shaky hands wrote the words, but your heart heard every one.

Did I tell you the comfort I felt as I traveled my final road? And the love I felt from your gentle hands that bathed and fed me, my dearest daughter, when I no longer could do it for myself? I turned anxiously as I entered the golden gates and watched you ring the bell. The bell you tirelessly answered every time with a tender smile and a gentle touch. Forgive me for slipping away in the dawn of early morning, my beautiful daughter, as you laid your head down to sleep, but you would have never let me go.

It was time.

Remember the day we kissed the Blarney Stone, my eyes twinkling with the wonder of Ireland? You gave me that memory and so many more, my treasures through the years. Thank you, my dearest daughter. Now—you live your days; fill them with as much joy and happiness as I did.

May the road rise to meet you,
May the wind be always at your back,
May the sun shine warm upon your face,
The rains fall soft upon your fields
and, Until we meet again,
May God hold you in the palm of His hand
-An Irish Blessing

OH! Did I mention? Heaven is every bit as beautiful as my Ireland.

I love you, Sue...E

Acknowledgments

A very special thanks to Kristi Brown of Tulip Hill Winery in California (www.tuliphillwinery.com) for taking the time to answer my questions. Your help is so appreciated. Congratulations on the opening of your new tasting room in Nice, California, in April 2004. If it is anywhere near as beautiful as your Desert Oasis Tulip Hill at The River in Rancho Mirage, it will be a winner!

A heartfelt thanks to Debra Butler of the CUA for all her support and encouragement. Friendship is truly a wonderful thing! And to the mini "Claim Jumper" lunch group!

Last but certainly not least, the publication of *Threads of Destiny* was truly a team effort. Thanks is simply not enough to express my gratitude to Stacia Seaman the editor, Sheri and her creative talent, and Kathy and her crew at StarCrossed Productions. You all made this happen.

J.P. Mercer
www.jpmercer0818@yahoo.com

CHAPTER ONE

The mind is its own place, and in itself
Can make a Heav'n of Hell, a Hell of Heaven
Satan, in John Milton's *Paradise Lost*

The baleful shadow of night lengthened its fervid fingers, chasing the light of day into the cold darkness of Sonora, Mexico. For *el andar muerto*, the walking dead, it did not matter; for them, no longer did the radiance of the sun warm their skin. For these forgotten ill-fated souls, the dying amber of another day meant another perpetual night of euphoric agony. They were mercifully unaware of the cold that pebbled their pale skin or the razor-sharp rocks that cut into the soles of their bare feet or the gnawing hunger in their bellies as they were prodded like cattle, naked, into the camouflaged huts. The oblivious, desolate cries of suffering and agony fell upon deafened ears. Their mindless, decaying bodies existed only as slaves to *El Serpiente* and *la cocaína de diablos*—until the white powder ravaged their spiritless bodies, consuming forever their wretched souls.

The crushing tentacle wrapped around the neck of the emaciated semblance of a man with lifeless eyes. Without a sound, his hand absently reached to touch the smooth leather as it tightened, shutting off his air, collapsing his windpipe. His rapidly beating heart, eager to leave its hellish existence, stopped before he sank to his knees, his hollow eyes staring into the nothingness his life had become. No longer an "obsequious follower to the secular parody of humanity," his insignificant, naked body lay unclaimed as the forsaken enslaved filed silently past.

Beads of sweat trickled down the faces of the two stultified guards. One twitched nervously as he watched *El Serpiente* out of the corner of his eye. Each man was terrified that any movement would summon upon them the wrath of the devil. The crack from the split tongue of the whip over their heads left both men trembling, choking on the taste of their own fear. The taunting, cold-blooded voice sliced through the stone-still air, forewarning.

"Clean this up. This one was weak, he didn't last long. Replace him quickly or you will take his place."

With stiff, jerking movements, the two men forced their frozen limbs to move. "*Sí, Jefe,* it will be done."

El Serpiente focused his dark, scrutinizing eyes on the pure, uncut white powder. "You are behind on production. Put some of your own men on the tables and send a few out tonight to pick up new recruits. Don't raid the villages; tell them to isolate the stragglers trying to cross the border. Have them wear their uniforms. If anyone cares if they come up missing, the focus will be on the Mexican *policía.*"

His face took on a rancor of evil, his voice a malignant sneer as he repeatedly pounded the handle of the whip into the palm of his hand. "I am tired of the woman. She has lost her fight. Get rid of her and deliver me a new one." He unfurled the whip, posturing it across the ground menacingly.

The guard flinched; the blood in his veins ran cold as he prayed to a God that had forsaken them all.

The private Learjet blended easily into the wispy feather-shaped clouds, leaving Mount Lemmon and the Santa Catalina foothills behind, soaring toward the coastal paradise of Santa Barbara, the American Riviera nestled at the foot of the Santa Ynez Mountains.

Staring absently into the white nothingness that mimicked her life, Cara Vittore Cipriano reflected upon the events of the past year that found her sitting alone flying toward California.

She had left Arizona that morning after completing the sale of her home in Tucson. For months, the sale had been pending, awaiting her return to the country. She had been en route to the East Coast when she had received a call from Maurillio Cervantes,

Cipriano Vineyards' vintner and her grandfather's oldest friend. His pleading voice, imploring her to come home, telling her that her grandfather had suffered a stroke and that she was needed, stunned her and without a moment's hesitation, she diverted the private jet westward to California. She couldn't shake the inauspicious feeling that she was in a race against time. She retrieved the cell phone from her briefcase and flipped it open, but hesitated—just as she had every other time she'd tried to call Jake over the past year.

Her thoughts on Jake, Cara laid her head against the glass, staring out the window at the quickly changing terrain of the Sonoran Desert to the populated coast of California. Every waking minute she felt the ache and loss of the woman she loved. She felt the threads of guilt and her past tugging at her heart as the Learjet changed altitude and circled out over the Pacific for approach to the Santa Barbara municipal airport.

The same cold hand gripped her soul as it had that day she'd stood on the bluff as her brother Stephen was lowered into the ground—into the land they both loved. The land that nurtured their youth and gave life to the grapes claimed Stephen's lifeless body. Slowly closing her cell phone Cara whispered, "Forgive me."

"May I refresh your drink, Ms. Cipriano?"

Cara answered without taking her eyes from the window and the endless sea of regret. "No, Anna. I'm fine, thank you."

Her mind replayed the two events that had changed Stephen's, Maggie's, and her own destiny forever—the week just before she had left for Harvard and the last time she had come home to Cipriano.

Cara had just received her degree in law and was excited and looking forward to going home. Home to Santa Barbara and the gentle, rolling hills laced with vines of sugar-laden grapes that promised the nectar of the gods. She missed the intoxicating bouquet of the wine and the oak aging casks that mingled with the ocean breezes permeating the air of Cipriano. She missed and longed to hear the sound of her grandfather's voice as he spoke of his vision for the virgin wine country. The look of love in his eyes and on his face when he stood each morning at dawn gazing out across the land to the grapevines was forever etched into her memory. It was time to go home to Cipriano to stand beside her grandfather as padrone *of the land they both loved.*

Sebastian Cipriano and Armanno Santini both grew up in the province of Cuneo in Piedmont in northwest Italy, an area rich in tradition of world-class vineyards. Both worked by the sides of their fathers, who passed down the tradition and secrets of Italy's finest wines to their sons. The desire to create an award-winning wine instilled in each by the passion and love for the grape.

The enigmatic Armanno Santini, in the eyes of the corporate world, was the successful CEO of the international Santini Imports. Santini Vineyards was his respite, a sanctuary for his family, away from prying eyes and the dangers of his world.

The three youths were inseparable growing up; Stephen adored Maggie and hero-worshipped his big sister.

Cara's heart eased at the sound of the happiness she heard in Stephen's voice when he called to tell her Maggie had accepted his proposal and that they were getting married as soon as Cara got home. It had long been expected that Cara would marry Robert Santini, Maggie's brother and heir to the Santini fortune and vineyards—a marriage her grandfather and Armanno Santini had arranged when both Cara and Robert were children. Stephen's announcement that would join the two families absolved both Cara and Robert of that duty.

From the moment on the beach in Maggie's arms the summer before she started college, Cara knew she was not destined to marry Robert or any man. Robert, who kept in touch, was just as relieved, and agreed to tell both families together when she arrived home.

As the hum of the jet engine hurled her closer to the past, echoing memories out of the haunted recesses of her mind tumbled one after another like dominos.

The summer before Cara was to attend Harvard Law School, Stephen was taking a summer enology classes at the University of California-Davis studying viticulture. Cara and Maggie spent their days together dreading the end of summer, when Cara was to leave for Cambridge. The last weekend of summer vacation, the two girls planned a day of riding and a clambake at the beach.

14

*"Last one to the old piece of driftwood has to dig the pit,"
Maggie yelled to her as she snatched up the burlap sack filled with
clams, jumped on her horse bareback, and raced headlong down
the beach. The soft summer breeze and the Pacific surf sprayed
playfully against her bronze face and body. Magdalene Santini,
the only daughter of Armanno Santini, was, to put it quite simply,
magnificent. The original girl from Ipanema, with long slender
legs that disappeared into a perfect waist. Her unusual light blue
eyes, framed by sun-kissed brown hair, accented golden skin that
glistened in the sunlight.*

*It was the time of day when the setting sun cast an ephemeral
light upon everything it touched. Gentle waves lapped at the shore
while sea birds floated on invisible currents. Maggie lay beside
Cara on the warm sand, taking in the boundless sky as stars began
to appear.*

*"I can't believe you will be gone in a few days. I'm going to
miss you terribly. What will I do without you?"*

*"It won't be forever, Maggie. Besides, you have Stephen. He
already follows you around like a puppy dog. Hey, look," an
excited Cara yelled, pointing to a falling star. "Make a wish quick,
and it will come true."*

*Maggie shut her eyes, crossed her fingers, and rolled over
onto her stomach, leaning on her elbows to face Cara. Even in the
faint, dusky light of sunset, Cara could see Maggie's blue eyes
darken as she whispered in her ear. "You could make my wish
come true."*

*She felt the pull of Maggie's eyes, like an ocean current
effortlessly dragging a struggling swimmer down deeper into its
depths. Her heart stood still as Maggie's words sparked a
sensation that raced down her spine ending in an inferno in her
groin.*

"It isn't Stephen I want, Cara Cipriano. It's you."

*The dawn of another day found Maggie in Cara's arms as
they huddled under a blanket on the beach. The only warmth was
from each other and the last of the dying embers in the campfire.*

"Will your mother be worried, Maggie?"

Maggie cuddled closer to Cara, afraid that she was on the verge of crying. "No, she knew I was with you and would probably spend the night at Cipriano."

An emotional Cara held Maggie's hand, her heart aching, knowing it would be the last and only time they would ever be together like this. "I suppose we better head home."

Through her own misty eyes, Cara gently traced a tear as it ran down Maggie's cheek. "Please don't cry, Maggie. I can't bear to see you cry."

Maggie lifted Cara's fingers to her mouth and softly kissed them. "I will never be sorry for last night, Cara Cipriano." She knew as Cara did what was expected of her and that what her heart wanted would never be allowed.

That single night. There on an empty stretch of beach, both young women had willingly given their virginity to each other under a blood-red moon. That one night of sweet, youthful abandon changed the threads of destiny and exiled Cara behind emotional walls.

Anna's friendly voice interrupted her bittersweet journey into the past. "We'll be landing in a few minutes, Ms. Cipriano. The two cars you requested are standing by; one will take you to the hospital. Mr. Cervantes asked me to apologize for not meeting you and to tell you he would see you at the hospital."

Her immediate thought was that her grandfather's condition had taken a turn for the worse. "Did he say if my grandfather was all right or if his condition had changed?"

Anna smiled, trying to alleviate Cara's anxiety. "Ms. Cipriano, the last we heard he was doing well."

Cara eased her tense body back into the seat. "Thank you, Anna. Will you please prepare the luggage so there will be no delay departing the plane when we land?"

"I knew you would want to get to the hospital as soon as you could, so that has all been taken care of, Ms. Cipriano. Can I help you with anything else?"

"No, Anna, that will be all. Thank you."

CHAPTER TWO

The elevator stopped on the third-floor ICU of the Santa Barbara Cottage Hospital. Cara stepped into the dimly lit corridor and hurried through the double doors past shadowy figures and rooms with unfamiliar sounds of pinging machines toward the circular nursing station. A haggard-looking man dressed in scrubs glanced up from a row of monitors.

"Hello, can I help you?"

"I'm Cara Cipriano. Can you tell me the condition of my grandfather, Sebastian Cipriano, and what room he is in?"

Before the man could answer, Cara heard Maurillio's familiar voice. "Cara! *Bambina amata,* you are here! Come, we will talk, but first I will take you to see your grandfather."

When she reached his room, Cara inhaled deeply and hesitated nervously as she entered the darkened hospital room, focusing her eyes on the still figure of her beloved grandfather lying in the bed. The sight of his frail body, so pale and vulnerable, caused her to lean against the door frame for support as she felt the strength in her legs weakening. One side of his face drooped in a formless pose as oxygen assisted his breathing and multiple bottles of fluid infused through tubes attached to his body. As she stood in the shadows, unabashed tears ran down her face and a sob caught in her throat.

On unsteady legs, Cara slowly crossed the room and stood helplessly looking down at her grandfather. An unbearable ache and ineffable warmth filled her heart as she gathered his thin bony hand, the hand that had guided her so lovingly through the years, to her trembling lips. Her eyes followed her fingers as they combed through silvered hair, and she wept for all the lost years and the losses in her life. She wept for Jake and for Stephen.

"Oh, Grandfather, I do love you so and I am so sorry. Please forgive me."

Cara sat in the dark, feeling the aloneness known only by those who have abandoned their beliefs. Maurillio's soft voice and gentle touch to her shoulder reminded her that she had come home for yet another reason, and she was about to find out why.

"Come, Cara. You are tired. I will take you home. We will talk on the way." The old foreman's gentle eyes could not disguise the tempered steel in his voice when he added, "And then I have something I must show you, *Padrone.*"

The rising sun was beginning to lighten the horizon over the gray expanse of the Pacific Ocean. Cara leaned her tired head back against the seat, allowing the muffled sound of the waves to soothe her as they drove along the winding stretch of coastal road that would take them to Cipriano Vineyards. Vine-covered hills gently sloped as far as the eye could see. Grape-laden vines with their outstretched arms seemed to be welcoming Cara home.

As they drove past a field of Petite Syrah grapes, it saddened Cara to remember the day the first vines were planted several years ago. It was her and Stephen's project, and they had worked alongside each other planting the new vines.

Maurillio instinctively knew what she was feeling. "You have blamed yourself long enough for Stephen's death, Cara. It is time to let it go."

Cara's eyes clouded with regret. "You don't know what happened, Maurillio. I was responsible for Stephen running off the way he did the day he died. If only I had—"

Maurillio interrupted her. "I don't know what happened, Cara, but I knew what was between you and Maggie long before you left for college. Anyone with eyes could see Maggie loved you as Stephen loved her. You cannot change the past. All you can do is to go on with your life. Your grandfather needs you now, more than ever. Strange things have been happening, and he has not been well long before this stroke."

"Strange things? What are you saying, Maurillio, what things?"

"Accidents, new workers that do not have a care about the grape or the quality of the wine or the reputation of Cipriano. I found something by accident this morning, Cara. You need to see."

"What about Paolo and Giancarlo? Paolo has taken responsibility of the daily operation, has he not?"

"Your older brother Paolo, yes, he did assume the responsibility of daily operations, and Giancarlo oversees the business end. But *malocchio* lurks in the shadows. Something is not right, Cara, and after this morning I think I know what. We need to find out who is responsible."

Cara reeled at the implications of Maurillio's words. He stopped talking a moment, then stammered, "There's more, Cara."

Cara turned her tired eyes toward Maurillio and held her breath, bracing herself, praying for the inner strength to deal with it.

"It's Maggie. She has married and has a daughter who is five years old."

Shock registered on Cara's face. "Five years old? Maurillio, Stephen died just over five years ago. Oh my God! Is the child Stephen's?"

Maurillio's weathered, worried face brightened when he spoke of the child. "Oh yes, Cara. She is without question Stephen's."

"How long has she been married, Maurillio? Is she happy?"

Maurillio's eyes lost their smile and the hardened look on his face alarmed Cara. "She married three years ago. I am sorry—your grandfather did not want you to know. He forbade anyone to tell you. The child is your niece, Cara. And as much as she looks like Stephen, she looks just as much like you."

Cara was dazed as she tried to process all that Maurillio was telling her. *Maggie was going to marry Stephen because she was pregnant? Did he know? Oh, Stephen, what must you have thought when you walked in and saw Maggie and me together the morning of your wedding?* The torment in her heart was too much to bear.

She asked one last question as they drove along the road through the vineyards leading to Cipriano Villa. "What is the child's name, Maurillio?"

"Sebastiana Vittore Cipriano." A proud smile beamed from Maurillio's face. "But she has chosen to be called Tiana."

The staunch Cipriano foreman directed the driver to take the luggage into the main house, and after Cara had checked to see that her assistant had settled in comfortably, she joined an anxiously waiting Maurillio. As she approached him, she noticed for the first time how old he looked.

Maurillio's gentle voice forced away the memories of happier times. So many years. Had it been that long? "Come, I need to show you something."

Memories and their ensuing emotions continued to assault her senses as she curiously followed Maurillio to the cavernous aging room. He led the way to the area where the wine barrels slated for recycling were stored. They would be sold at a very low percentage of what they originally cost, but the practice enabled smaller wineries to have access to quality barrels.

"I signed for a shipment of new barrels and thought it was a duplicate, so I pulled the receiving papers. There was not a mistake. I also checked the purchase order to see who signed it."

"Who, Maurillio?"

"It was my signature, Cara, but I did not sign the order. The barrels had been ordered to replace ones that were soon to be recycled. I came here to check on a shipment of the recycled barrels to a winery I was not familiar with."

Cara listened intently and watched expectantly as Maurillio retrieved a small crowbar from a shelf and pried the top off one of the barrels, revealing a hidden compartment.

"And I found this." He reached inside to retrieve three black plastic bundles. "I found several more in other barrels, too." He reached into his pocket for a knife and slit a small hole in one of the bundles.

Cara's hand trembled as she wet her little finger and brought the white powder to her tongue. "Cocaine?" A hard look crossed her face. "Who is doing this? Who is involved in this, Maurillio? Does my grandfather know about this?"

"It would kill him, Cara."

Maurillio fell silent. Cara's sharp mind deduced what Maurillio wasn't saying, her brown eyes deepening to almost black. "Which one? Which one of my brothers has done this?"

"I wish I knew. I suspected something—too many accidents, and then all the late shipments. Paolo is in debt, gambling. He spends far too much time in Vegas away from his wife. Giancarlo lives well beyond his means; too many women and fast cars, expensive suits. Life at Cipriano has changed much since you left, Cara. It is not what you remember. Then, with your grandfather's ailing health—more changes. And now the stroke and on the heels of that—this." He gestured to the white powder.

Outrage seethed under the surface as Cara replaced the bag and repositioned the top of the barrel. Then with dead calm, in a voice that had put fear in many an opponent in the courtroom, she said, "I am home now, Maurillio, and I will make that unquestionably clear. I am assuming control of Cipriano, and I will find out who is behind this. But for now, let's keep this to ourselves."

The loyal winemaker shifted uncomfortably from one foot to the other. "Cara, there is one more thing I need to tell you."

She eyed the old man with an uneasy feeling as he continued.

"Maggie and Sebastiana live here at Cipriano. Maggie is married to your brother, Paolo."

CHAPTER THREE

Cara stood in the mist of dawn on the terrace between her room and what once had been Stephen's room looking out over the forever beauty of Cipriano. Yesterday, Arizona, everything seemed so far away, so unattainable. She tried to push thoughts of Jake from her mind, but it was as impossible as holding back the breath she took. She reached into the pocket of her jacket, wrapping her fingers around a crumpled paper that burned into the flesh of her fist. Dr. Larkin's words of a year ago were scorched forever into her memory.

"Cara, your preliminary HIV test result is positive, but we won't know for sure if you are infected with the virus until we get confirmation with additional testing.

"Keep in mind, please, a positive HIV test result does not mean that a person has AIDS. But because some reactive test results may be false positives, every reactive rapid test must be confirmed by a supplemental test, either Western Blot or immunofluorescent assay, IFA. It usually takes three to six months for a person to develop detectable antibodies, so I will test again in three and six months."

Dr. Larkin leveled his tired eyes on Cara's unreadable stone face. "In the meantime, you should take precautions to avoid transmitting the virus."

He paused a moment to allow Cara to process what he had just told her before going on. "I also ran a HCG level. It's routine in situations such as this."

Cara blinked her eyes in question, then in realization. "A pregnancy test?"

An eternity passed as she held her breath, waiting for him to continue.

"It was positive."

Cipriano and her grandfather needed her now. What Maurillio had shown her and told her weighed heavily. She was the one Grandfather had chosen to succeed him at Cipriano. He had taught her with love and patience, entrusting to her the family and the heritage of the grape—Cipriano's lifeblood. Cara reflected back to a time when, as a young woman, she had stood in the same spot many times in the early predawn light mentally preparing herself for the day she would assume the responsibilities of *padrone*. She had vowed to make her grandfather proud by caring for the land and the family.

Oh God! Stephen was going to be a father. She could hear his voice from when he was a small boy. *Cara, take me with you. I won't get in the way, I promise.* She could still see his face, anxious and pleading to let him tag along. How many times had she been touched by his love as he ran to the fields to find her, so excited about his latest find or with a skinned knee for her to kiss and make better?

After their parents died, Cara had found herself acting as both sister and mother to her little brother, giving rise to the intense bond that had formed between them. She would never forget the look on his face, first confusion, then hurt, the morning he and Maggie were to be married when he'd burst into Cara's room and found Maggie lying in her arms. He never knew it was two dear friends simply sharing memories.

A small voice startled her and she looked up to see, sitting on the steps, a child who could have been her at that age. Dark hair and eyes, tall for her age, she was dressed in blue jeans and scuffed boots.

"Why are you so sad? Are you my Aunt Cara? My mother said you would come. Are you going to stay?"

Cara chuckled, "And just who might you be?"

The girl stood and stretched herself as tall as she could, then in a very grown-up voice announced, "I am Sebastiana Vittore Cipriano. But you may call me Tiana, and I am going to be *padrone* one day."

Cara cocked her head, raised an eyebrow, and smiled as Tiana defiantly blurted out, "Grandfather told me so. He said I was just like you!" Then she turned and ran down the stairs, disappearing around the house toward the kitchen door.

Cara could smell Cook's special blend of coffee before she entered the kitchen. Standing at the stove stirring oatmeal was Hattie—short, rather plump, now graying Hattie. The name and face were chicken soup for Cara's soul. Hattie had begun working for Cipriano well before Cara's birth.

The look on Hattie's face when Cara walked into the kitchen and stole a freshly baked cinnamon roll was precious. Both acted as if she had not been gone a day. "If I've told you once, I've told you a thousand times, Cara Cipriano, you will wait until breakfast is served and sit down at the table like normal people do to eat."

She dabbed at her eyes with the corner of her apron. "Now get on out of here and let me do my work." Her voice cracked ever so slightly as she pointed to Tiana, who had her mouth and both hands filled with cinnamon roll. "And take this other hooligan with you."

Cara bent over the small woman and kissed her gently on the cheek before reaching down to pick up the five-year-old child. "It's good to see you, too, Hattie."

Tiana, her brown eyes wide with uncertainty, held tightly to Cara's neck as they crossed the yard. "Where are we going, Aunt Cara?"

When Cara reached the front of the stables, she sat Tiana on a workbench and looked at her with undisguised love in her eyes and heart. "If Grandfather says you shall be *padrone,* you shall be. Today I will start to teach you. But first do you think I could have a hug? I need one very much right now."

Maggie watched the scene from her window, taking in the sight of her daughter and her best friend. There had never been a doubt in her mind that the two would bond and share the same deep affection and love that she, Stephen, and Cara had. She smiled as Tiana put her arms around Cara's neck and hugged her. *I wouldn't have thought it possible. She is even more beautiful the older she gets.*

"What's so interesting out the window, and where is Sebastiana? You just let her run wild with no discipline."

Maggie turned to face her husband, who stood in the doorway. "I didn't hear you knock, and you're not welcome in my bedroom, Paolo. Tiana is my concern, so you needn't bother yourself as to her whereabouts."

The six-foot, muscular man crossed to where his wife was standing, his tanned face twisted in anger. Maggie could smell the rank odor of alcohol that clung to his breath as he grabbed her wrist and sneered, "In case you've forgotten, Maggie, you're my wife, and I have a right to be in your bedroom and a right to be in your bed if and when I so choose." He twisted her arm behind her back and pulled her up against him. "Maybe you need another reminder."

Maggie's free hand landed a hard slap across Paolo's face, leaving a mottled imprint and angering him even more. Pinning both of her hands behind her back, he roughly covered her mouth with his. He had forced her before, but never without a fight. Struggling to free herself, Maggie bit down as hard as she could, drawing blood from Paolo's lip. The coppery taste of his blood mixed with the taste of sour bourbon sickened her.

He grabbed the front of her blouse, ripping it open. "You know I like it when you want it rough. We'll see how much fight you have left in you when I'm through fucking you!"

Maggie stifled a scream, knowing that if Tiana heard her she might come running in—and that was the last thing she wanted. Paolo's breathing was quick and hard as he drunkenly struggled with the buttons on her jeans when an angry voice demanded, "Let her go, Paolo."

Arrogantly, he looked to see his sister standing in the doorway. "Well, if it isn't the family lesbian returned! Pardon me, my mistake, the favorite son. You should have waited to see how it's done, Cara. Oh, I forgot. You've already seen and done our little Maggie here, haven't you?"

Cara's eyes were on fire. Her fingers curled into a fist. Her body was taut with rage. "I said, let her go...now, Paolo."

He snickered and released Maggie. "Be my guest. Maybe she'll put out for you, it wouldn't be the first time."

Cara started for him, but Maggie was faster and used her body to hold Cara back as she begged, "Please, Cara, Tiana might come in. Let it go, please."

Paolo stormed out of the room, slamming the door behind him.

Humiliated and embarrassed, Maggie turned away from the questioning eyes of her best friend. "I'm sorry you had to see that. It was ugly."

Cara reached out and gently turned Maggie toward her, holding her hands, turning them over to inspect the bruised wrists. "Does this happen often, Maggie? He abuses you?" A sudden frightened look crossed Cara's face. "Does he abuse Tiana?"

"No, mostly he just ignores her, and she stays away from him. If your grandfather were here, this would never have happened today."

"And you? He abuses you, Maggie?"

Maggie could not bring herself to look Cara in the eyes.

"I promise you, it will never happen again." Cara's face softened. "She is beautiful, Maggie. I've met her; she has your spirit and Stephen's innocence and love for the land."

Maggie's eyes filled with tears for the loss of one and the return of another. "Yes, she is beautiful. I just wish..."

Cara pulled Maggie to her breast. "Oh, Maggie, I do, too. He would have been so very proud of her."

Maggie clung to Cara, gathering strength from her being home again, feeling safe as Cara's protecting arms tightened around her. She cried tears of hope as Cara stroked her hair soothingly.

Cara spoke softly. "Come, I want you to meet someone. Then we will join my brothers for breakfast—it is time for everyone to know I am home."

Cara's return to Cipriano was not an easy one. Both brothers resented her. Grandfather returned home paralyzed on one side and unable to speak. He sat, expressionless, in his room overlooking the vineyard, seemingly unaware of the people and

J. P. MERCER

activities that went on around him. Paolo, whose resentment of Cara had grown from childhood, felt it was his right as eldest son to take over Cipriano when his grandfather stepped down. And Giancarlo, who had visited Cara once when she had been at Harvard and never returned after learning of her lifestyle and preference in lovers, remained coolly detached and indifferent to her presence.

Days turned into weeks, and Cara threw herself into every aspect of running Cipriano Vineyards. She was up before dawn every day and was the last to leave the fields at night. No matter how busy she was, she made time every day to watch over Maggie and Tiana. She would put the little girl in front of her on her horse, and the two would ride between the endless rows of white and red grapes or wander through the cool, cavernous aging room. Every night, Tiana waited for her Aunt Cara to tuck her in with a bedtime story as an inseparable bond grew between the two.

Cara closed the book, then lifted the small girl's head off her shoulder and onto the pillow. She eased off the bed, leaning over to kiss the sleeping child's cheek good night. She was tucking the covers around her shoulders when she felt Maggie's hand on her back and heard her whisper.

"I checked on Stephen. He's all settled in, sound asleep." Maggie grasped Cara's hand, kissed her daughter good night, then pulled Cara from the room and led her across the hall to her bedroom. Maggie's eyes studied her friend a moment.

"You've been working too hard. You need more rest, Cara, three or four hours of sleep a night isn't enough. But I do have to admit, breast-feeding agrees with you. You have that new mother radiance about you."

Pointing to the open door of the veranda and two comfortable-looking loungers, Maggie directed Cara to sit as she walked toward the wet bar to pour two glasses of Merlot.

"Maggie, do you mind? No wine while I am still breast-feeding. Besides, I'm tired, and if I have the wine I will never make it to my room tonight."

Maggie was about to say something, then thought better of it. "Iced tea?"

28

The two friends sat under a night sky that was lighted by a sea of luminous stars that merged into the darkness beyond. They enjoyed their drinks and each other's company as they listened to the muffled, distant sounds of the surf lapping against the rocky shoreline.

When Cara raised her hand to her neck, trying to stretch out the tightness, Maggie sat her glass down and stood beside her. "Lean forward a bit, and I'll see what I can do to loosen up those muscles."

Cara chuckled softly. "Oh God, remember how I used to tense up before the swim meets, and you would stay up all night working on my neck? Those trophies should have your name on them, you know."

Maggie smiled, remembering those nights. After Stephen died, Cara never came home again. And even though they hadn't kept in touch over the years, Maggie had kept track of her and knew Cara had become a reputable attorney. She wondered what Cara had left to come home and sensed there was something that she regretted leaving behind.

"You are a beautiful, caring woman, Cara. How is it that you never found someone to share your life with? You can't tell me you don't have them lined up knocking at your door."

Cara closed her eyes; she was tired, and the longing for Jake was too close to the surface as Maggie's hands manipulated the sore muscles of her neck. She imagined that the gentle hands touching her were those of the hazel-eyed doctor. Every night, Jake shared her dreams. Each night, she heard Jake's soft moans and felt her smooth silken skin against her own. She missed all that was Jake, all that touched and warmed her heart.

She winced as Maggie hit a tender spot; at the same moment, a jagged sense of loss pierced her soul. She couldn't tell Jake what had taken her away from her, and she couldn't explain why she had to stay in California.

Maggie's gentle voice interrupted her thoughts. "Hey you, still there?"

Cara swallowed the lump in her throat but couldn't hide the pain from her best friend.

Maggie sat down beside her. "I see the sadness in your eyes, Cara, and I know there is more behind it than the situation here. I know you as well as I know myself. You've been home for weeks now, and I can see and feel your pain. The only time I see those beautiful brown eyes of yours smile is when you are with the baby or Tiana. The guilt over Stephen's death and the question in your eyes when you look at your grandfather is eating away at you. Whatever else it is, I know you are suffering." Maggie reached for Cara's hand. "I'm here, my dear friend, if and when you want to talk about it."

Cara held Maggie's hand like a lifeline thrown to someone trying to escape a sinking ship. She knew that she eventually needed to tell Maggie the whole story about Jake, and Mexico, and how the baby was conceived. And the reason she'd run away from it all. But for now she had to concentrate all her efforts on keeping her family and the vineyards safe. She was responsible for finding out who was sabotaging Cipriano to run drugs.

Not a day passed when she didn't want to pick up the phone to call Jake. She wanted to tell her every detail of every minute from the past year and that she loved and needed her more than she needed air to breathe. Too many ghosts kept her silent.

CHAPTER FOUR

Jake was on edge and irritable and was having a difficult time concentrating on work or anything else as she looked at the date on the calendar. *A year ago today.* Cara had just up and left the ranch to go back to Tucson—without so much as a good-bye or an explanation. Jake had attempted to contact her, had left numerous messages. All had gone unanswered. Then one day the phone had been disconnected.

Cara had been sullen and withdrawn after the operation in Mexico. At first, they had lovingly nursed each other. Jake tended to the burns that Sandro had inflicted on Cara's body with a cattle prod, and Cara soothed Jake's bruises and emotional trauma. Each caressed the other, not in passion, but with love and a desire to ease the heartbreak of betrayal. Cara's gentle touch opened the portal to Jake's soul. From it, a beacon of warmth and light had radiated outward from her very essence. She realized the depth of her love for Cara and knew that life without her would be unbearable.

When Cara left her bed to sleep in the guestroom, it devastated her. Jake suspected post-traumatic stress syndrome and encouraged Cara to talk to her or someone about the ordeal, but every time she attempted to bring the incident up, Cara tensed up and avoided the subject—shutting her out, refusing to discuss any aspect of the time in Mexico.

No one denied that the unsanctioned operation in Mexico had been a success, although Sandro had escaped. After months of back-breaking investigation and analysis of the bits and pieces of evidence from the brutal murders of young Hispanic women whose bodies had piled up in the morgue, Jake knew the face of a killer. It was the face of a trusted friend.

For months, at the end of each day, Jake walked into the ranch house expecting to see the beautiful, enigmatic lawyer. Yet each night, only echoing silence greeted her. She grew keenly aware of the deafening sound of her loneliness amid an overwhelming sense of abandonment. As days turned into weeks, she became increasingly worried and confused. She crawled into her bed at night exhausted, but sleep would not come. Her bed, as well as her heart, felt empty without Cara. The mournful howl of a lone coyote echoed the same tormenting question. *Why? Where is she?*

Jake had gone over every possible reason she could think of why Cara would simply disappear without a note or a call. As each ponderous thought drew a blank, her heart hardened a bit more.

This day was no different. Long before the sun rose, she got up, tired and sleepless, and went into Nogales to finish the notes she had neglected these past months. Morning dragged into afternoon as she struggled to concentrate on the latest stack of reports Kalani was tying up on the Jane Doe deaths that needed Jake's signature.

Jake closed the file she was holding and exhaustedly looked at her watch. "Kal, I'm due at an INS hearing to help secure green cards for Lupe and her father."

Kalani studied her friend's haggard face. "How are they doing? It's been darn near a year now." Kalani knew as soon as the last word was out of her mouth that she had opened a festering wound. "I'm so sorry, Jake. Have you ever heard from her or anything about where she is?"

Jake faltered momentarily, then paced the length of the room to the window, her eyes fixed on nothing but the distance. "No, Kal. I never did."

At a loss for something to say, Kalani simply moved to Jake's side, putting her arm around her and rubbing the small of her back. "I'm sure if something were wrong, she'd have gotten a message to you."

"I tried everything, letters even, hoping they would be forwarded, and phone calls to her home and her office in Tucson. They didn't know or wouldn't tell me anything. I even went to her home up the canyon. The caretaker told me the owner was gone indefinitely."

Jake leaned her exhausted body against her friend. "I finally used a friend in the Bureau, against all policy, and all I got was that she was out of the country."

"It's time you let her go, Jake, and get on with your life."

"I know, Kalani, and I'm trying." Jake looked at her watch. "I'm late for the INS meeting," she said, then solemnly turned and walked toward the door, knowing her heart would never let go.

CHAPTER FIVE

All morning, Cara had been in the northern field overseeing the planting of the new Sangiovese vines along the trelliswork. She stopped and straightened her back, surveying the work with a faint smile, then brushed the freshly turned earth from her hands and pants. *Grandfather will be pleased*, she thought. After she told the workers to break for lunch and then continue with the planting, she walked back to her Jeep and headed for the aging room. She planned to draw samples from the barrel-fermenting Carneros Pinot Noir, seventy-five casks of private label that promised to be a gold-medal-winning vintage.

As she drove she reached for her cell phone, remembering that she'd meant to ask Maurillio about certain years' harvests and an odd entry she'd noticed when she was reviewing the books the night before. Something about the figures didn't feel right, and the thought had been surfacing in her memory all morning long. When Maurillio answered, she asked him to meet her and to bring his crush reports from the past five years.

With the thought still fresh in her mind, she drove up to where a grinning Maurillio stood waiting for her. He puffed out his chest as he proudly announced, "It is a good morning, *Padrone*."

Cara rolled her eyes hiding a threatening smile. "Please, Maurillio. Cara, remember?"

Maurillio smiled and nodded. In his mind she was *padrone* and always had been. In his heart, he knew that Cara coming home was a good omen.

"Do you mind gathering the drawing equipment while I get the books from my office? I want to ask you about something."

"As you wish, *Padro*—uh, Cara."

Maurillio was curious as he went about gathering the equipment she had requested. He arranged his crush reports on the long worktable at the end of a stacked row of fermenting barrels of wine, then siphoned off the samples Cara requested. When he finished, he joined her at the table as she was comparing his reports with the entries in Cipriano's books.

"Maurillio, please start with and read me the tonnage from 1998 on."

The natural earthen-cool room echoed with Maurillio's accented voice and Cara's suspicions. When Maurillio finished, he sat quietly while she carefully compared the two documents again—his numbers against Cipriano's books. There it was, a noticeably lower yield than Maurillio's figures indicated.

"Your figures, are they your entries only?"

Maurillio had a questioning, knowing look on his face. "I have always kept my own figures, Cara, this you know. Your brothers tell me it is old-fashioned to do so and that computers are more efficient, and maybe that is so. But I have done it this way since the old country, when your grandfather and I did it by the light from the oil lamps in the field. It is my way."

"The tonnage from the year 2000 on, your records show they were as high as '98 and '99?"

Maurillio's eyes scanned down his handwritten figures and the tonnage totals.

"Do you remember, when you harvested, was there a noticeable decline in the crush those years, Maurillio?"

"No, Cara. In fact, Cipriano had perfect weather, and they were good harvest years with exceptional quantities."

Maurillio's face creased in a frown as he studied the figures more closely. "As I told you, strange goings-on. I suspected there was a discrepancy between what I saw crushed and our profit for those years, but this is the first time since your grandfather's illness that I have been able to made a comparison between my figures and theirs."

"What it shows, old friend, is that someone has been doctoring the books, possibly since 2001."

Deep in thought, Cara stood and leaned against a stacked pallet of barrels as she spoke. Feeling a vibration, she turned her head to look up, then quickly swiveled her head back to Maurillio to see his eyes widen with surprise. The barrels had come loose and were falling directly toward them.

Heedless of his own safety, Maurillio moved as quickly as his aging body allowed, lunging for Cara. Neither was fast enough. Both were pinned under the cascading barrels, pressed in by a mass of wood and wine. Several barrels broke open, spilling a river of red and anointing them, as a ritual, a baptism of evil to come.

Cara clawed to get out from beneath the barrels, then frantically moved the crushing weight off the old man's chest. Kneeling beside the fallen foreman, she held his head and lowered her ear close to his mouth while desperately searching for a carotid pulse along his neck. Maurillio wasn't breathing, and she couldn't find a pulse. Cara had known CPR since she was a teenager and responded quickly. Carefully, she positioned his head and neck and breathed into his mouth.

Just as she started chest compressions, two workmen who had heard the barrels crashing to the floor ran into the aging room.

Between breaths, Cara gasped, "An accident! Maurillio is not breathing. Call 911!"

Frantically, she continued to try to revive Maurillio as precious seconds ticked by. Pausing between chest compressions and assisted breathing, she searched for a pulse. "Please, Maurillio, breathe, just breathe! I won't give up until you breathe!"

Just as she heard the wail of approaching sirens, Maurillio sucked in a ragged breath and opened his eyes. Dazed, struggling against the crushing pain in his chest and legs, he tried to speak. "No accident..."

"For God's sake, Maurillio, don't try to talk. Help is on the way!"

Cara rode in the ambulance to the emergency room, holding Maurillio's hand in a death grip the entire way. After he was out of immediate danger and had been transferred to the ICU, Cara was on the phone to Washington calling in a favor.

The day after she found the cocaine in the wine barrels, she had contacted an old friend and Harvard classmate, Rachel Slade, who was now with the attorney general. Rachel's office was already well aware of the Rivera drug cartel's Santa Barbara connection. Various Justice Department agencies had been following the traffic from Mexico to California and Arizona for some time. They knew the drugs were being warehoused in many locations in California and Arizona before being moved across the country to be cut and distributed. The trail of white led to Santa Barbara's wine country, as well as to the exclusive residential area of Montecito. The accident in the aging room made Cara fearful for everyone's safety at Cipriano, especially her family's.

"Rachel, there's been an incident since we talked. Seems whoever is behind the drug connection is getting a bit nervous now that I am home."

Cara rose from behind the oak desk and walked over to the window, her eyes gazing out across the sprawling green lawn and the picnic area.

"What happened?" Rachel asked.

Cara combed her fingers through her hair as she recounted the incident. "My grandfather's best friend and vineyard master, the man I told you about who found the drugs, Maurillio Cervantes, was caught under several wine barrels that mysteriously just rolled off the rack. Rachel, he's been my grandfather's right hand for years. He came to this country with him after my parents were killed in an accident."

Rachel's concern was audible. "I'm so sorry, Cara. How is he?"

"Maurillio could have died, Rachel. Thank God, he suffered no serious internal injuries, but it's serious enough. Both legs were broken and his pelvis was crushed. It was no accident. Those barrels didn't come loose by themselves." Glancing out at Tiana, she shuddered as she thought about the danger her family never suspected.

"The drugs are here, and they are tainting and endangering the lives of my family. The situation is simply unacceptable. I need help, Rachel."

Rachel breathed heavily before speaking. "Cara, at the risk of breaching protocol, all I can tell you is that it's in the works as we speak. We could make some arrests now, but it would be the little guys and we would blow months of the hard work we've racked up trailing the big guns in this operation. Arrests now would snare a handful of runners and stop a few drug shipments, but by the next morning they'd have twice that amount ready to hit the streets."

As Cara listened patiently, in her mind's eye she saw the innocent faces of her family, and she vowed she would do whatever it took to protect them. Their safety and the reputation of the winery—their livelihood and legacy—all were at stake.

"I understand this is an ongoing investigation, and I understand that you want the top-dog bastards, but I have a family to protect and a winery to run. What makes it worse is the fact that one of my own brothers might be behind this."

Rachel took a deep breath. "I'll make a call. I know the FBI is already looking at a damn fine agent to go undercover at Cipriano. And this agent knows the wine business to boot. Perfect cover. Give us a day or so to coordinate our DEA and FBI field operatives and brief them, Cara. Just keep your eyes open and be careful."

"Thanks, Rachel. This nightmare can't end too soon for me."

"I know, my friend. I hate that you have to go through this, but we are one step closer to nailing them and shutting them down. Oh, and just to set the stage there, you need to announce that you are hiring a new employee to replace Maurillio. This may sound cold, Cara, but Maurillio's accident gives you a legitimate reason to replace him while he recovers."

Cara sighed, then pressed her fingers against her temple in an attempt to lessen the throbbing there. "As much as I hate to admit it, you're right. I'll do what I have to here, Rachel, but please get that agent here soon."

Cara returned to the window where she looked out at Tiana, who was still romping on the lawn with the dog while Maggie sat in the swing between two huge oak trees, holding the baby. Cara's heart swelled with pride and love as she watched her family through the window.

The collie suddenly assumed a defensive posture, her hackles bristling as she locked her eyes across the way toward the stables. Cara followed the dog's watchful gaze to Paolo, who was followed closely by Giancarlo. They were engaged in what appeared to be an argument. Throwing up his hands, Paolo stalked into the stables and Giancarlo calmly turned and walked to the garage and sped out in his new silver-blue BMW.

As she observed her brothers' display, Cara voiced her suspicions aloud. "The dog doesn't trust one of you. Is it you, Paolo? Or you, Giancarlo? Or both? Well, no matter, because I will not allow it. Never assume that blood is that thick, dear brothers. And God help you if either of you is involved."

CHAPTER SIX

Jake sat on the porch of her ranch house, gazing out as a yearling frolicked in the pasture. The stress of the past year had taken its toll. She had gone through a kaleidoscope of emotions that had drained her energy and destroyed her trust. The realization that Cara had simply vanished from her life was difficult to accept. The words spoken, the love shared, it all meant nothing now. Her mind filled with the empty sounds of empty words that had tumbled from Cara's mouth in the guise of what she had called "truth" that now battered the heart she had opened to Cara's professed love—only to have it devastate her world with its own enfeebled truth.

Never trust anyone other than yourself, Jake. She vowed, sitting on the porch that day, that no other person could ever hurt her that way again. *Damn you, Cara Vittore. Damn you to hell!*

When Sam had died, Jake thought her world would never right itself. They had been arguing for weeks. Sam wanted to get married, to start a family, but she wasn't sure that was what she wanted. The night before he died she'd told him she was taking an assignment on a serial killer task force in Washington state and that she needed time to sort things out. It was one of their worst arguments, ending with her sleeping in the guest bedroom. The next morning Sam left without saying good-bye, taking the keys to her Jeep. He was blown to pieces in her place.

Later, it was discovered that a convicted murderer and drug boss connected to the Rivera cartel was responsible. Jake's work and testimony had helped put him on death row. When the guilty verdict was read, he'd turned to Jake with eyes as cold as death itself and raised his handcuffed hands to point to his head with his index finger and thumb. A paid informant who had linked the drug boss and the bomb was found hanging from a billboard that said Fight Crime, his tongue cut out and his hands cut off. It must have sent a powerful message, because the authorities never again heard as much as a murmur.

Jake carried the guilt of Sam's death, and when her dad was murdered, she couldn't find the way to survive the loss. She had collapsed, unable to work. When she came home for her dad's funeral, she stayed.

She was back at work and beginning to reconcile the loss and recover when she had first laid eyes on Cara Vittore. Then, on the witness stand testifying as an expert witness for the state, Jake had reeled backward as the confident lawyer slashed her testimony to shreds. After that, Jake blamed the arrogant defense attorney for a mistake she herself had made processing DNA evidence for the murder trial. Her error led to a mistrial and subsequently a not guilty verdict.

Two years later, their paths crossed again. Jake still despised the egotistical attorney, who had been retained to represent a young soldier arrested for the mutilation and murder of a young Hispanic woman who had left her home in Mexico to cross the desert illegally into Arizona. Cara had been thrown into an ongoing investigation of the murder, one Jake suspected was the work of a serial killer.

To use the simple cliché "oil and water don't mix" would have been an understatement. Sparks flew and ignited a flame in both women's hearts. They fell hopelessly in love, and together they survived the harrowing showdown with Jake's close friend, Sandro, in Mexico—only to have Cara walk, without explanation, completely out of Jake's life.

The loss and betrayal of both Cara and Sandro devastated her, penetrating deep into the dark place of her soul she had struggled to survive ripped her heart out and left her bleeding all over again. She turned her feelings inward, building impenetrable emotional walls to shut down the memories and all the empty places Cara had left.

Jake moved through her days with the determination of those who seek forgetfulness, throwing herself into an ever-increasing workload, requesting more field time and additional training from the drug enforcement training facility at Quantico. Whatever the job, it didn't matter, nor did the level of danger. Jake's closest friends, Matt Peyson and Kalani Trujillo, could only stand by helpless and watch her going full-speed through the motions. She pushed herself to the brink of mental and physical exhaustion, maintaining a relentless pace. Nothing anyone did or said slowed her down or influenced her from the grueling pace she set for herself. She lived at the morgue and at the Phoenix FBI training facilities when she wasn't following every lead or rumor that might reveal Sandro's location.

Jake had arranged for a day to improve her accuracy with her new M-1911 pistol on the outdoor firing range at the FBI's Phoenix headquarters. The special grips she'd ordered felt good and fit well in her hand. She flipped the safety off, then aimed at the tight black circle in the center of the target and emptied the full magazine. The action was smooth; even with slight movement, most had hit dead center. She started to reload when she felt the vibration of her pager summing her to the office of the special agent in charge.

"Please come in, Jake." SAC Josh McNeil got up from his chair behind his desk and motioned to a small table with coffee and sandwiches.

Jake wondered what the SAC had on his mind and took a minute to gather her thoughts.

"Can I pour you a cup, sir?"

"Nope, I've had enough today to jangle my nerves effectively for a week or more. But please help yourself."

McNeil sat on the edge of his desk and reached for a folder as he spoke. "Your file shows you know the business of wine making."

Jake looked at McNeil with curiosity.

"I have an assignment for you. I think you're what we need here." He handed her a folder containing the particulars of the operation and the specifics of her role. Jake scanned the documents as McNeil continued.

"I believe—and the assistant director in Washington agrees— that you're perfect for this assignment. You would be working undercover special ops on a task force created to permanently eradicate the key figures in a Mexico-based trafficking organization. You'd be joining a special task force comprised of agents from FBI, DEA, ATF, Customs, and Immigration. Phoenix and Tucson have historically been major points for cocaine smuggling and distribution. A large percentage of it enters the country, as I am sure you are well aware, through the notorious Nogales storm drain system. Last year, there was a noticeable decline in those shipments due to our beefed-up concentration on these areas."

Jake's brow furrowed with interest as McNeil continued. "We know the points of origination in South America as well as the transit points in Mexico, primarily in Sonora. But when the preferred smuggling routes into the United States began to change, and we observed a significant decline in seizure quantities, we started to wonder. Then we discovered a startling piece of information. According to interagency intelligence and surveillance assessments, the cartel is slipping under the radar, as it were. Big time. They have clearly established connections in California's wine industry, specifically in vineyards from Santa Barbara on up to Napa Valley."

McNeil walked behind his desk and sat down, leaning back in his chair as he talked. "We've had no idea which or how many vineyards were involved in California, but we had the list narrowed down to four possibilities. A recent development at one of the most prestigious vineyards reduced that list to one. Your experience as part-owner of a vineyard and your knowledge of wine making made you a prime candidate for the job."

He paused, trying to read Jake's reaction. "Agent Biscayne, shall I continue?"

Jake listened intently to the SAC's briefing. After Sandro had been exposed and confirmed to be *El Serpiente* and the *jefe* of the drug pipeline across the Mexico border, Jake's close friend and colleague, Matt Peyson, had connected the trail of murdered, mutilated women from the Persian Gulf to the Sonoran desert to him. Jake and Matt had both pledged to follow any lead or trail that would lead to Sandro.

Jake knew all too well that the desire for revenge could be a detrimental emotion, but that one motivation kept her going. She knew now the connection between Sandro and the Rivera drug cartel. It was what her father had been working on when his trusted friend, Sandro, had slipped a garrote around his neck from behind, taking his life.

The timing couldn't have been better. The Sonoita vineyards' Petite Syrah entry in the San Diego national wine competition provided Jake with indisputable credentials and a perfect cover, and an unfortunate accident at a California winery had opened the door the rest of the way.

Jake stood and walked across the room to look out the window at the deep orange sun coming up over Camelback Mountain. A moment later she turned, a grim, determined look clouding her hazel eyes. "When do I start?"

CHAPTER SEVEN

Cara's return to Cipriano Vineyards had been bittersweet. She never questioned her responsibility; she loved her grandfather. Her child, Tiana, and Maggie were her family now. Paolo's sullenness was now a relentless, open resentment. It was growing steadily, and he had taken to directing much of his animosity toward his wife and stepdaughter. As a result, Cara was constantly going up against him. Her days were long, but the nights were never-ending hours filled with longing for Jake.

As exhausting as her days were, however, she never allowed her grueling schedule to interfere with seeing to her grandfather's daily care. Every morning, Cara went to her grandfather's room. She liked to talk to him as he worked with the therapist, telling him about what the day held for her in the vineyard and the winery. Then again at lunch, after she fed Stephen, she would try to join him as he ate with Tiana and Maggie. Every day she waited for some sign, some response that he recognized her. At times, he would turn toward her with a question in his eyes. The first time he did it, she enthusiastically greeted him—only to see the blankness return.

Most of the time, he seemed unaware of her presence, or anyone else's, except for Tiana. When she burst into the room daily, chattering away as if nothing was wrong and playing around his chair, a tiny smile infused his eyes as they followed her every move. Then she would settle in and talk to him in such a way that it seemed as if the two were sharing a secret.

Cara paced down the spacious hallway leading to her grandfather's rooms, once her parents' rooms, on the south side of the Tuscan-style villa. Her father had designed the wing himself, carefully detailing the placement of tall, panoramic windows facing south, east, and west, having declared that no day began properly unless he was holding his wife in his arms as he awoke to the rising sun or ended properly if he wasn't watching the sunset while in her embrace.

This morning she wanted to talk to the physical therapist about her grandfather. As she entered the room, her heart leaped in her chest with excitement and she raised her trembling fingers to her mouth. Grandfather was standing alone between the parallel railings, taking small steps, his right leg shuffling forward as he struggled to move his left leg into position. He had made tremendous progress in the past few weeks, going from being bedridden and confused to taking his first steps. Cara felt tears of happiness welling up in her eyes as she watched his shaky hand sliding along the rail as he took his first unassisted steps.

She stepped back for a moment to wipe the moisture from her cheeks, then smiled and walked to her grandfather. "Good morning, Daniel. Grandfather, I am so proud of you!"

Sebastian motioned with his unaffected hand to Daniel for his wheelchair. Daniel chuckled and raised his eyebrows, positioning the wheelchair in place for Sebastian to sit.

"And a good morning to you, Ms. Cipriano. If your stubborn grandfather keeps up this pace, he'll be back in that winery of his in no time," Daniel said enthusiastically.

Cara hugged her grandfather before she knelt down to lift his foot onto the footrest of the chair. "He does seem to be making great progress these last few days."

"Indeed he does." Daniel patted Sebastian's shoulder. "In fact, I have some equipment I need to bring in, Ms. Cipriano. If you are going to visit for a while, I can go get it and start setting it up for tomorrow."

"Yes, go right ahead, Daniel."

As Daniel exited the room, Cara pushed her grandfather toward the east window so he could feel the sun. She pulled a chair near him, then took his impaired hand in hers and began a series of massaging motions the therapist had shown her that would help the circulation. As she manipulated each finger, she told him about Tiana's romp on the lawn that morning with the dog and Hattie's latest attempt to keep them all out of her kitchen on baking day. She thought she saw a bit of a sparkle in his eyes when she told him the state of the newly planted vines on the north slope. As she spoke, her mind kept wandering to her latest suspicions about her brothers, neither of whom was overly thrilled with the fact she had hired a replacement for Maurillio.

She hadn't realized she had stopped talking as she thought about how the situation would affect her grandfather if he knew. She continued to stretch and pulled the muscles of his hand and fingers; then, sensing his eyes on her, she suddenly felt as though her thoughts were exposed. She patted his hand and stood up. As she moved to leave, he clumsily clasped her fingers in his weak grip.

Cara was afraid to move as she raised her eyes to meet his, which did not look away. There was an unspoken moment of recognition as he held her gaze. She raised her hand to his cheek, stroking his freshly shaven skin. The look Cara saw in his eyes was peaceful and filled with love and acceptance. She never tried to hide the tears of happiness or the bright smile on her face.

"I love you, Grandfather."

A few seconds passed, then he squeezed her hand in response.

"I promise to do my best, Grandfather. I cannot change the past or the terrible events that have happened. But know this: Cipriano Vineyards, your legacy, shall remain strong and prosper."

The old man raised his hand to her face, his shaky finger caressing her cheek. She looked to see, for the first time, a faint smile. She wept and pressed against his hand.

Cara saw his jaw open, saw his drooping mouth working to form a sound.

"Caa-raa," he managed to say with much effort.

"Oh, Grandfather."

His eyes filled with tears as he struggled to shape each syllable. "Baa...by...you...rs?"

Cara's chest constricted. She knew the time had come. *Please, Grandfather, please understand what I am going to tell you.*

Her grandfather stared blankly beyond Cara as she held his hand and told him the entire story of Jake and Mexico and how Stephen had been conceived.

Her eyes filled with tears and her voice broke as she went on, "I love Stephen, Grandfather. He is the most precious thing in my life now. I ran from Jake to get an abortion out of the country. I didn't want a child that was conceived of violence and rape. I tested positive for HIV, and my world collapsed. I wanted to die. I was full of anger and fear. I loved Jake with every fiber of my being, but I couldn't risk exposing her."

Cara took a breath trying to calm her trembling voice and body. "I couldn't go through with the abortion, but I agonized with my decision every day until I was tested after three months and again when I was six months along."

Cara felt her grandfather squeeze her fingers. She looked into his tear-filled eyes as he struggled to form the words to tell her he loved her and baby Stephen.

With the utterance of those simple words, she knew he had forgiven her for Stephen's death. "The tests were negative, Grandfather." She gathered the old man in her arms and whispered. "I love you, too."

Still cradling his frail body in her arms, Cara could see his exhaustion as she eased him into his bed. She propped his left side with pillows, then pulled the covers over his shoulders and kissed his cheek as she smoothed his hair back, listened to his peaceful breathing as he slept.

As she gazed at her grandfather, she saw the man who was as a father to her. She sighed, her face reflecting an inner peace that had long been absent from her heart. Finally, she sensed that she had finally come home. Their lives had come full circle.

"I will not disappoint you. Never again."

She drew the curtains and started to leave. It was then that she ran into Hattie, crying as she stood by the door holding Sebastian's lunch tray.

"Child, I never thought to see this day."

Wiping the tears from her face, Cara took the tray from the old woman and hugged her.

"Neither did I, Hattie. Neither did I."

CHAPTER EIGHT

"That new foal is coming around," Matt offered nervously. "Uh-huh, sure is, strong legs, just like her mama."

Matt reached into the cooler for a Corona and wiped the sweat from the bottle. "You think the Syrah has a chance at the show?"

"It will compete in the best of class gold or silver, and it will speak for itself. It's a darn good wine, Matt, and the visibility presenting it in San Diego will help my credibility and establish my cover."

"I have a bad feeling about this assignment, Jake. We, uh, I, well...Kalani and I were thinking maybe you should take a break and maybe pass on this one."

"I promise I will, just as soon as this job is done. This task force has made a significant difference in the flow of drugs into this country, especially Arizona, and it might lead us to Sandro."

Matt tensed at the sound of Sandro's name, but he didn't voice the fear that was gnawing in his gut. He had something to tell Jake and it had to be done right.

"How's Maria, Matt? I miss having my morning coffee with her when I'm away. She is a special lady."

"She's quite the woman, isn't she? You and I both know how much this mess with Sandro has hurt her, far deeper than she will ever let on. But she just keeps going."

"I know, Matt. He meant the world to her—to all of us. Sometimes when I go by the café, I see her just sitting, staring at the empty places on the wall where she took down all the pictures. It has to be so hard for her."

Matt nodded.

"Matt, you never make small talk, and you're as nervous and fidgety as a yearling colt being halter trained. What's on your mind?"

"I, um, well..."

"Matt, spill it. What's up?"

"Jake, you know how I feel about you, but I've accepted the fact that you—well, that what I want for us just won't ever be. So I guess that waiting around for you to see things my way, um, well, I, uh..."

"Matt, whatever it is you need to say, just say it, before it's tomorrow already."

"Jake! I'm dead serious here."

Jake leaned back in the rocker and gave Matt her full attention. "All right, Matt, what has you all riled up?"

Several seconds passed while Matt rallied his courage.

"If it's okay, with you, I, um...asked Kalani out on a date."

Jake burst out laughing. "Is that all this is about? All this schoolboy hemming and hawing just because you want to take Kalani out!"

Matt's face turned several adorable shades of red. "Well, you know she's always been interested. We even dated a little while you were in Chicago."

"Why didn't you keep seeing her?"

Matt sputtered out a nervous laugh. "Seems I took a fancy to some damn spitfire of a doctor. Anyway, I was trailing after you so much I could never see anyone else for long. But lately we've been spending some time together and..."

Jake waited for Matt to continue. When he didn't, she asked, "And what, Matt?"

"This morning she came in the café while I was having coffee. All serious like, she said, 'Matt Peyson, you and I need to have a talk.'"

Jake could see the intensity in his eyes. "Go on, Matt, I'm listening."

"Like I said, we dated some. We, um, kinda..."

Jake was having a hard time understanding what Matt was trying to say. "Kind of what, Matt?"

"Damn, let me just say it, Jake! It was just once, the day your dad told me you were engaged to Sam. I guess once was enough."

Jake's eyebrows scrunched in confusion. "What's that supposed to mean?"

"Teresa is my daughter, Jake."

Jake was at a loss for words. Finally, she reached for Matt's hand. "Oh, Matt, I am so sorry for everything. I never knew, she never told me either."

"Yeah, said she didn't want me by default or out of some misplaced sense of guilt or obligation." He trailed off, scrubbing his chin as he always did when he was thinking.

"I'm not proud to say this, but it's how it went down. She made a big show out of dating other guys, so when it was obvious she was pregnant, I never even thought, just assumed. Oh hell, Jake, she was never promiscuous, you know that and I should have, too."

Jake stood and faced the one man who was truly her friend. Putting her arms around his neck, she hugged and held him. "Kalani would never lie about something like this, Matt. If she says Teresa is your daughter, she is. You both are my dearest friends, and I love you both. I should have made you realize long ago that my feelings for you were of deep friendship and never could be romantic. Maybe if I had faced and admitted my sexuality, you and Kalani would have been raising your daughter together all this time. Matt, I still don't know if I am attracted to women or if it was just one woman. But the past can't be undone. All we can do is go forward."

She pushed him back so she could look into his blue eyes. Holding his handsome face between her hands, she said, "Now don't you have something better to do with that carcass of yours than to hang around here with me? Go!"

"Jacquelyn Lee Biscayne, you are one hell of a woman. Who ever gets that heart, be it man or woman, is gonna be one lucky SOB."

Matt stood, leveled his hat on his head, and started for his truck. As he stepped out into the yard, he turned back to look at

Jake framed in the doorway. *Cara Vittore has no idea what she walked out on.*

In his heart, he knew he would never love another woman as he did Jake. But he was ready to start his life, and his heart ached a little less as he thought about his daughter and Kalani. He turned on his heels, jumped in the truck, and sped toward his future.

The phone rang, but Jake, absorbed in her work, made no attempt to answer it. Kalani, who was working at her own desk, shook her head and got up.

"Yes, she's here. Hold a moment, please." Kalani put her hand over the mouthpiece. "Jake, it's McKenzie Quinn on line two for you."

Jake looked up, a bit puzzled, then took the phone from Kalani. "Hello, McKenzie."

"Jacquelyn. How are you?" McKenzie asked with an Irish lilt.

Jake hesitated, not knowing what to say to McKenzie. She hadn't seen or talked to her in over a year. She had liked McKenzie from the first words they shared and regretted that their friendship hadn't continued.

"McKenzie, it's nice to hear from you. How is everything going for you? Are you all settled in?" Jake paused awkwardly, thinking about the night when she'd met McKenzie in the lounge of the hotel she was staying in. It was the night she'd learned that McKenzie and Cara had been lovers, the same night that a drug bust had gone wrong at the border and Matt's partner, Alejandro, had died at Sandro's hands. "I thought you might have...uh, well, that you went..."

McKenzie knew Jake was referring to Cara and was struggling to ask her if she was with her.

"Jacquelyn, I haven't seen Cara since that night at the hotel in Tucson. Now, if I am remembering right, you owe me a lunch date, love. Shall I drive down to Nogales or do you want to come to Tucson?"

Jake put an elbow on the desk and tiredly rested her chin in the palm of her hand as she considered her choices. Here or there? She'd known the first time she'd laid eyes on the redhead that she definitely could be a force to reckon with.

"We are so busy here, McKenzie. Plus, I've been traveling a good deal for the Bureau. I just haven't the time, but maybe in a few weeks."

"Well, then, it sounds like a bit of fun is just what you might be needing, and you did promise to take me for—ah yes, I remember, authentic Mexican food. Now, you've heard about the stubborn nature of the Irish, I'm sure. Well, let me tell you, it's all true. I refuse to take no for an answer."

Jake chuckled as her mood lightened. "Why doesn't that surprise me?" She raised her eyes to see Kalani mouthing "Go."

With both women trying their best to convince her, Jake finally relented. "All right, on one condition. My friends call me Jake."

McKenzie's voice lightened even more. "Deal. I look forward to seeing you again—Jake."

"I'll be in Tucson tomorrow. We could meet about three at the Radisson...Good, see you then."

Kalani, who had not intended to eavesdrop, could not contain her pleased smile when Jake agreed to have lunch with McKenzie. *Getting out with a friend may free her mind of the past few months and do something for the sadness that constantly colors her eyes. At least for a while.*

At two-thirty the next afternoon, McKenzie Quinn was sitting at the Radisson Hotel bar visiting with Rebecca, the hostess catching up on the latest news as she waited for Jake to arrive. Nursing a gin and tonic, she wondered why Cara and Jake weren't together. She hadn't really lied to Jake about not seeing Cara—she hadn't, but she had talked to her on the phone a few times during the past year and it was strictly business. Cara refused to discuss anything else, effectively shutting the door in McKenzie's face, especially where Jake was concerned. McKenzie knew how it felt to have loved and lost the dark beauty, but looking at the attractive blonde woman walking toward her now, she knew without a doubt that Cara was the loser this time.

"Hi," a voice edged with slight modesty said, disturbing her reverie.

McKenzie paused to survey the extraordinarily appealing woman standing at her side. Jake was a study in understated beauty, dressed simply in khakis and a white silk shirt. *Simply breathtaking.* McKenzie remembered how attracted she had been to Jake as she perused her lean body, hazel eyes, and wind-tossed blonde shoulder-length hair.

She felt a flush of warmth when her eyes betrayed her appreciation and enthusiastically reached for Jake's hand. "Jacquelyn, you truly are a sight for sore eyes." She laughed, her green eyes smiling.

"Jake, remember?"

"Well then, Jake, shall we find that little cantina you promised that that has the best food this side of the border?"

Over lunch McKenzie and Jake caught up on everything, from work to McKenzie's new apartment to how everyone in Arizona will tell you how you will get used to the extreme heat of an Arizona summer because "it's a dry heat."

McKenzie wondered what had happened between Jake and Cara. Her instincts told her the sadness in Jake's eyes had Cara written all over it. She decided to chance it and just ask. "Have you heard from Cara?"

Jake's face hardened as her head snapped up from her food, her hazel eyes flashing. Her words were calm and measured, betraying an array of mixed, confused emotions beneath them. "McKenzie, it's a touchy subject for me, and if you don't mind I'd rather just enjoy lunch and not explain it."

McKenzie knew Jake was going through the motions of being polite as she absently pushed her food around on her plate and made poor attempts to pass off her half-hearted smiles as genuine. He voice held an edge, and McKenzie felt the conversation and mood between them had definitely changed. She regretted asking about Cara and she tried to catch Jake's eye.

Unconsciously, Jake turned her head to avoid McKenzie's gaze, but not before her eyes unveiled a well of pain.

McKenzie reached across the table and slid Jake's hands into hers. "I'm here if you need to talk."

A tear betrayed Jake as she looked at McKenzie. "Thank you, Kenzie, but please, let it go."

She attempted a recovery with a not very convincing laugh and none-too-subtle subject change. "Now, are you going to let that Corona sit there and go flat while you keep jabbering?"

"Heavens, no, but it isn't a Guinness. We wouldn't want to start a rumor about the Irish not being able to hold their liquor, now, would we, love? Actually, I thought we might order a pitcher of margaritas and stay through dinner."

Jake laughed, allowing McKenzie to change the subject. The other woman's warm, easy way was relaxing, and to her surprise, Jake found she was genuinely enjoying the afternoon.

By midweek, McKenzie's restlessness and distraction had become intolerable, and she realized she wanted to see Jake again to possibly explore the attraction she felt toward her. She called Jake's office only to discover she was at the winery. McKenzie cancelled her afternoon appointments, jotted down Kalani's directions, and set out for Sonoita. When she arrived at the vineyard, a very surprised Jake greeted her with an undeniably welcoming smile. They spent the rest of the day together, roaming about the winery and picnicking on cheese and wine under a huge spreading oak tree at the top of a knoll that stood sentinel over the vineyard.

Over the next few days, Jake found she looked forward to McKenzie's company. She enjoyed the companionship and presence of the intriguing Irish woman. Jake felt comfortable with McKenzie, whose open and friendly personality was exactly what she needed.

One evening, after a day of riding and exploring several antique and craft shops, Jake impulsively invited McKenzie to accompany her to the wine competition in San Diego.

"We can go a few days before the show. We'll stay at the Hotel del Coronado, which has an incredible ocean view and sparkling stretch of white sand beach."

McKenzie agreed, and as they stood beside each other on the porch of Jake's ranch watching a spectacular Arizona sunset, Jake stiffened at the feeling of McKenzie's hand on the small of her back. Not that McKenzie was undesirable—quite the opposite—

but the touch seared through her as the memory of Cara's touch exploded across her skin.

"You're a beautiful woman, Jake." McKenzie reached up to gently stroke along the curve of Jake's cheek with her finger.

Jake turned her eyes back to the multilayered colors of the sunset. "Kenzie, I—"

"Please, let me finish. You are as beautiful on the inside as you are on the outside, and a very desirable woman. I don't know what happened between you and Cara that put the sadness in your eyes. And I know you're not ready for anything serious now, but if and when you are, I will be here."

Jake continued to gaze toward the horizon, her hazel eyes lost in memory as the setting sun painted the sky in a palette of passionate red and orange. McKenzie's heart felt the pangs of hope and desire when Jake interlaced their fingers as the last remnants of light sank into the clouds, igniting them a deep crimson.

"Can you accept being my friend for now, Kenzie?"

ON

J I stop wondering and missing her? When will I stop wanting her?

As the soft evening breeze gently caressed her face, she closed her eyes, and in her mind's eye she saw Cara leaning against the doorway, barefoot, in her dad's shirt, brown eyes smiling, reaching out to steal her heart. Jake loved those eyes, especially how they glistened and swirled with specks of gold as they made love. A knock on the door chased away the image, bringing her back to the realization that Cara was no longer in her life.

Stepping back into the room just as the door opened, Jake simply looked on as McKenzie waltzed into the room with two spa attendants in tow. One pushed a cart laden with cheeses, wine, candles, a variety of oils, and thick white towels, while the other carried a massage table.

McKenzie waited, rather pleased with herself, noting the look of surprise and confusion playing across Jake's face as she watched the attendants. One scurried about the room, meticulously creating a romantic ambience, placing and lighting candles and preparing the wine and cheese while the other positioned the massage table on the private balcony, covering it with pearl-white silk sheets.

"You decided to have the massage here in the room?"

McKenzie's eyes turned radiant with joy as she laughed. "No, my dear Jacquelyn, you are!"

Jake's eyes showed her surprise, then her delight as she gave McKenzie a warm smile. "Oh! Kenzie, have I died and gone to heaven?"

The petite Irishwoman, her eyes focusing lovingly on Jake, handed her a body sheet, then gave a wink. "No, love, not yet. But ya know what they say, heaven waits for no woman, so go take your clothes off and enjoy a bit of heaven right here on earth."

Relaxed and basking in the tingling sensations from the massage and the wine, Jake wrapped the warmed cotton robe around her naked body and strolled out to the balcony. Once she was settled on the lounger, her eyes soon closed as the calming mantra of the surf, slapping on the rocks below, soothed her into a state of half-sleep.

McKenzie showered and put on her robe, refilled their wineglasses, then went to join Jake on the balcony to savor the peacefulness of the night. Leaning against the railing, she listened to the sounds of the tide rushing boldly across the sand and noted, across the bay, lights twinkling like tiny beacons guiding the seafarer to safe passage. She wondered why Cara had chosen to leave such an exceptional woman. Her eyes drifted to Jake's face. It was peaceful, the constant telltale lines of stress eased in sleep.

Jake had asked her to be her friend, and while she knew they would always be that, she wanted more. She thought of the irony of the situation. McKenzie had loved Cara, who wanted Jake, who loved Cara. She knew without a question that she undoubtedly was falling head over heels in love with Jake.

Finished with her wine, McKenzie set the glass on the table, then moved to sit beside Jake. Slivers of moonlight captured Jake's hair and played across her face and the smooth skin of her throat. McKenzie's pulse quickened as her eyes played across the seductive curve of a soft breast that was exposed slightly under Jake's robe. She wanted to touch, to feel, and to make love to every inch of this woman.

Hazel eyes barely opened as McKenzie's long fingers brushed a wisp of blonde hair from Jake's forehead. A shiver of need surged through McKenzie as she traced her fingers across Jake's cheekbone to her lips, memorizing Jake's jaw line with her fingertips.

Then as if in slow motion, she moved to brush her lips against Jake's ever so lightly. Jake stirred, and McKenzie heard a soft moan and felt the tremor of desire that passed through Jake's body and the quivering of soft lips beneath hers. She waited for the moment of uncertainty to pass, but when she felt Jake's arms encircling her neck, her tongue returned to trace sweet lips and found the warmth it sought.

She gently untied Jake's robe and ran her fingers along the silky skin and curves of a sculpted hip and waist to the outer edge of Jake's breast. She eased her own robe off and lowered her body onto the yielding softness of the woman beneath her, pulling her closer. She felt the undeniable shiver of passion as Jake's hips began to move against hers. She gently positioned her thigh and kissed Jake's eyes, then nipped at a tender spot below her ear. As her lips explored the incredible pleasure in the hollow of Jake's throat, she felt the urgency building like thunderclouds on the distant horizon, echoing her own building storm of desire.

She trailed feather-light kisses around firm breasts, teasing and taunting, avoiding the hardened nipples that ached to be touched. When Jake arched into her mouth, showing her need, giving permission, she licked and sucked each nipple gently. Her hands kneaded Jake's buttocks as their hips moved in a passionate rhythm.

McKenzie could hear Jake's breathing becoming shallower. Her own voice turned husky and filled with need as her fingers caressed the inside of Jake's thighs, brushing against the silky wetness they found there. "God! I want to touch and taste you. Please, Jake, let me make love to you!"

What McKenzie didn't hear as Jake opened to her was the name on Jake's lips. And the face in Jake's memory that was blurred by the tears in her eyes. One name. One face. *Cara.*

McKenzie woke, eyes still closed and with a smile on her face, and stretched, reaching to find that Jake's side of the bed was empty. Lifting herself up on one elbow, she listened for the sound of the shower running but heard only silence. A knock on the door interrupted her disappointment. She looked at the clock. "Sweet Jesus, it's after noon! Who is it?"

"Room service, ma'am."

Pulling the covers up over her nakedness, McKenzie yelled, "Come in, please."

A young man in a hotel uniform pushed a cart laden with fresh fruit and flowers through the door. Mouthwatering aromas of strawberries, mango, and quiche—and especially coffee—filled the room, eliciting a growl from McKenzie's stomach.

The young man took one look at the attractive, obviously naked redhead, then cut his eyes to the other bed that clearly had not been slept in. His boyish face blushed as he swallowed nervously and stammered, "Where—um, where should I set this up, on the balcony or—the other lady said to deliver lunch, uh, if you weren't down by noon." He handed McKenzie an envelope. "Oh! She said to give you this."

McKenzie laughed, knowing the picture the room clerk had running around in his head. *Guess it is every young man's fantasy, too!*

"Yes, please set it up on the balcony. And thank you." "Nothing but a boy," she mumbled and laughed quietly to herself as she gathered the sheet around her while he moved the cart to the balcony.

After his rather awkward retreat she sat, sipped her coffee and read Jake's note.

Kenzie,

If you're reading this, it must be lunchtime, so enjoy! Sorry, I had an early meeting this morning and a few things to do before the competition started. I left the rental car for you. Meet me downtown at the Westgate Hotel. We'll have dinner.

Jake

PS Thank you...last night was special.

McKenzie read the note again then raised a determined eye toward what promised to be a perfect day. A pleased, confident look crossed her face. *It's a start. I will help you forget her, Jake. One day at a time. We're good together, and after last night, I know I can make you happy.*

CHAPTER TEN

Jake's mind reeled with questions and doubts. Would she make the same choice in the light of day that she had in the dark of the night, out of need and in the throes of passion, to take McKenzie as her lover—to use her? Was it right to allow her bruised ego and battered heart to respond to McKenzie's honest touch? Knowing it wasn't McKenzie's face and green eyes she longed for, or her name on her lips as she reached orgasm, but brown eyes in the shadowy recesses of her mind beyond her reach that stole her passion?

When she entered the lobby of the Westgate Hotel, where the San Diego National Wine Competition was being held, she turned several heads—men as well as women—a paradigm of classic elegance and unpretentious grace. Her simple silk suit and blonde hair, casually gathered in a simple twist off her shoulders, perfectly accented her five-foot-seven lithe figure.

Jake was feeling the excitement and pride of having their Petite Syrah in the prestigious competition, but she also felt an odd uneasiness that was distracting. Her underlying objective was to be visible, establishing her credentials in the California wine scene as a reputable vintner. Her father had taught her about the grape and the making of the wine; she knew the language and was confident in her presentation and knowledge, but intuition had her looking over her shoulder.

As she exhaled deeply, her thoughts returned to McKenzie and the intimacy they had shared the previous night. She ran her hands across her skirt, hoping to settle her slight trembling and to calm the doubts running through her mind.

She made the circuit, stopping at the various tasting tables set around a large room off the private judging area. She sampled several excellent entries in the same class and competition that could possible give the Sonoita Syrah a serious run for the medal. She recognized many of the vineyard names, but some were as fledgling as hers and Matt's. Win or lose, she knew their Arizona wine would make a statement.

She was talking to a vintner from Northern California about the effects of the El Nino heavy spring rains and cool summer the year before that had caused a late start on their harvest when she felt a presence behind her. She turned to look into McKenzie's smiling face and warm green eyes, then blushed and shyly smiled back, her eyes meeting McKenzie's as the mental image of a naked McKenzie straddling her caused a flutter in her chest.

McKenzie gently caught Jake's fingers and leaned into her, brushing Jake's ear with her lips as she whispered, "Hey, I missed you this morning, love."

Jake smiled again, feeling a bit awkward with the intimacy. "Hmm, well, you were sleeping so soundly I didn't have the heart to wake you. Uh, did you enjoy your late breakfast?"

"Oh, yes, I have enjoyed this entire day and last night—especially you." McKenzie pulled Jake a little closer. "I hope you like California French cuisine and being pampered, because I made reservations up the coast for tomorrow night at the Miró at Bacara to celebrate, and tonight we're going to the Windjammer."

"The Bacara! Oh, it's beautiful there. How in the world did you manage that?"

"Ah, I will never tell my secrets."

McKenzie was very attentive as they walked around the event and Jake tried to concentrate, but her mind kept going through a mental checklist of McKenzie's attributes. *She's attractive, caring, fun, and a considerate, passionate lover. I enjoy her company, and she would be so easy to fall in love with and to care about.*

Those thoughts were interrupted by an announcement that the first round of judging would begin in fifteen minutes. Jake wanted to be at the table where the Petite Syrah was to be judged, so they made their way across the room.

Jake's eyes focused on a picture of a previous gold medal winner displayed on the wall behind the judging table. There was something so familiar about the brown eyes of the small girl looking up proudly at the vintner. The eyes reached out, beseeching her, but before she could move closer to read the name of the vineyard, she felt a presence and a touch on the back of her neck. Her heart pounded wildly against her chest and the motion in the room around her froze as an unseen force compelled her to turn. Her breath caught as her eyes locked onto the intense stare of the same familiar brown eyes that bored straight into her soul.

Alarmed, McKenzie saw Jake's face grow pale and heard the catch in her breath. Her eyes followed Jake's stare across the room to see her college lover and the one woman she knew Jake had loved.

Every muscle in McKenzie's body tensed as she possessively moved to stand beside Jake, placing her hand at the small of Jake's back. She could feel the fire in Cara's eyes from across the room as they exchanged looks. Cara Vittore was not going to intimidate her; forgoing any subtleties, McKenzie shot Cara a look that clearly conveyed her message to stay away.

When she felt Jake tremble and falter, she supportively put her arm around her waist allowing her to lean into her. "Do you want to go back to the hotel, Jake?"

Not taking her eyes off Cara, Jake managed a nod as the room began to spin.

The judging was about to begin and the chatter in the room slowed as McKenzie led Jake toward the exit. Before they could get through the main lobby, Cara, with Maggie in tow, intercepted them by the exit.

McKenzie stepped protectively in front of Jake, then with a seething anger said, "Not here, Cara. Just step aside so we can leave without an incident."

With a silent plea, Cara's eyes never left Jake. When McKenzie moved to go past, Cara softly questioned, "What do *you* want, Jake?"

Jake stood motionless as if in a dream, unable to take her eyes from Cara as McKenzie stepped forward and lashed out at her. "You have a lot of nerve, Cara Vittore. If you have an ounce of decency, you won't do this. Not here, not now. We are leaving. Enough!"

Throughout McKenzie's tirade Jake and Cara's eyes never left each other, both women lost in an eddy of emotion and unanswered questions.

Maggie took offense to McKenzie's tone and behavior and went to stand by Cara's side, trying to get a grasp on what was going on. She could see the turmoil and emotion playing on both women's faces and suspected they knew each quite well.

Cara finally spoke. "Jake, please, I need to talk to you. There are things you—I need to—"

McKenzie turned to Jake, waiting for her to respond, and when she didn't, McKenzie answered for her. "You need? This isn't about you, Cara!"

"Please, Jake, you don't understand. It isn't what you think. If you'll let me explain—"

"She understands more than you give her credit for, Cara," McKenzie said, the anger rising in her voice and flashing in her green eyes.

Cara's patience was waning. She felt herself losing control as her voice broke and cracked, and she ran a trembling hand through her hair. "This is between Jake and me, McKenzie. I made the only choice I could."

A small crowd began to gather, distracting McKenzie from her anger, and for the first time she focused on Cara and noticed the changes in her old friend, the weight loss and stress lines. Realizing this wasn't an arrogant Cara, but a woman whose voice was filled with hurt and frustration, McKenzie felt her attitude soften. She had loved this woman and she didn't want to hurt her with any more words said in anger.

"We all have choices, and whether we like it or not, we have to live with the consequences of our actions, right or wrong. You've hurt people, Cara, without even once considering that maybe, just maybe, your decision was not the right one and that someone else's life would be affected by your choices."

McKenzie's words broke through Jake's daze. "McKenzie, what—Cara, what are you talking about? Didn't have a choice in what?" Jake asked, looking to Cara for an answer.

Sensing Cara's distress, Maggie took her hand, knowing her friend was on the verge of a meltdown and couldn't handle much more. She directed her words to McKenzie and Jake.

"Whatever this is all about, it's not going to be settled here. So if you will excuse us, we have a five-year-old who never sleeps until she has a bedtime story read to her."

Both McKenzie and Jake were taken aback by the sudden intervention of the beautiful woman holding on to Cara's arm, taking charge of the situation and apparently of Cara.

Maggie's timely intercession was enough for Cara to regain her composure. "Yes, that's true; she won't. I'm sorry. This presumptuous intrusion on your evening is inexcusable. Please, accept my apologies."

With that, Maggie and Cara walked out of the lobby toward the valet parking. Both Jake and McKenzie stood, stunned, their gaze following the two women. Jake couldn't believe what had just happened and what she'd seen. Had she actually seen Cara? And with a woman?

CHAPTER ELEVEN

Cara shifted effortlessly through the gears of the yellow TR7 as she drove along the Pacific Coast Highway toward Cipriano. She hadn't spoken a word in over two hours, and Maggie could do nothing but helplessly watch her best friend's emotional turmoil. Cara seemed unaware that she was driving well over the speed limit, and as they approached Santa Barbara, Maggie reached over and covered Cara's larger hand with hers.

"Cara, honey, pull over."

Cara pulled off the 101 onto Milpas Street and drove the vintage sports car to an isolated spot on the beach alongside Chase Palm Park.

She buried her face in her hands. "I'm sorry, Maggie, for speeding, I don't know what I was thinking. I just—" Frustrated, Cara turned her head and with an anguished look of longing stared out across the ocean.

Maggie opened the door of the car. "Come on, let's walk a bit." She took Cara's hand and directed her to lean against a stone retaining wall. She bent down to take first Cara's shoes off, then her own. Cara's hand trembled in hers as they walked along the water's edge.

Maggie finally broke the silence. "Do you want to talk about it? It might help. I know the blonde was someone you cared a great deal about, and that something happened between you that caused you both a great deal of pain."

The expression of pain and sorrow on Cara's face confirmed Maggie's suspicions.

"Pain I caused, Maggie. It cannot be forgiven, and I can't change the past." A look of defeat, then acceptance crossed Cara's face as though the threads of destiny had been irrevocably cast.

As they walked hand in hand, Maggie reached up and brushed from Cara's eyes the strands of auburn hair blown by the ocean breeze. The scene at the hotel had shaken Maggie, leaving her uncertain and full of unanswered questions. She felt an undeniable aching in her soul; deep down in a secret place she rarely visited, she realized she had always hoped she would be the one Cara looked at the way she had looked at the blonde earlier.

When Sebastiana was born, it was Cara she had wanted by her side. The closeness they had renewed and shared since Cara's return, combined with the bond of love they had for each other's children, gave Maggie hope they would be together as a true family one day. She hadn't felt as complete and happy since Cara left for college.

Squeezing her best friend's hand in a gesture of reassurance and support, Maggie wished she had laid claim to Cara's heart years ago, before Cara lost it to another. Wrapping her arms around Cara's waist, she kissed her on her cheek, then grasped her hand and tugged her toward the car.

"Hey you, let's go home."

On the ride back to the hotel, Jake was quiet and withdrawn. When they reached the lobby, she said, "I need a little while to myself, Kenzie, is that all right? I have a meeting in the morning and I should go over some files tonight. I shouldn't be too long."

Disturbed by Cara's sudden reappearance in her life, McKenzie reluctantly agreed. She watched Jake make her way across the lobby until the elevator doors closed behind her.

It's not all right, Jacquelyn. It's not all right that you're shutting me out completely. Please don't put those walls back up. Let me help you through this. Damn you, Cara! How is it that you burrow under the skin and run hot in the blood of every woman you touch?

She remembered how she'd felt when Cara left her, first in Boston after college, then again years later in Tucson when she took a position at the same law firm Cara worked at, hoping they could rekindle their relationship.

McKenzie asked herself what it was about Cara that women couldn't forget. She ordered a drink, and by the third one, she remembered: Cara driving her crazy with need and her long legs wrapped around her waist.

When did I start asking asinine questions?

Jake found her way across the room by the soft light coming from the wet bar. She poured herself a brandy and went out onto the balcony, taking a deep breath in the hope that the cool ocean breeze would clear her head. The shock of seeing Cara still had her reeling, but the numbness was wearing off and an overwhelming feeling of hurt was taking its place, opening long-festering wounds. Her irrational emotions vacillated between jealousy and hate. *Whoever said that there's a fine line between love and hate must have been betrayed by a woman.*

When the picture of Cara making love to another woman invaded her thoughts, she poured herself another drink.

A child. Well, it isn't as if she got her pregnant. Oh God, she has you crazy. I feel like such a fool. Was Cara involved with her when we...? Was everything that happened between us a lie?

Jake remembered her first impression of Cara as a ruthless bitch. She had devastated Jake on the witness stand, making her look as if she were an amateur dabbling in DNA evidence. *No, I won't believe that—or is she?*

Exhausted, Jake finished her drink, then crawled into bed. *I'll give you my pain tonight, Cara, but tomorrow is another day, and believe me, I'll get over it!*

Jake was well aware of McKenzie's disappointment that they had not spent their last night in San Diego exploring what they had started the night before. Instead, she pretended to be asleep when McKenzie came into their room. Her heart went out to McKenzie, but it was not the time to start a new relationship. She had an undercover assignment that was potentially dangerous, and she didn't know how long the job would last.

Jake drove along the coastal highway toward Santa Barbara. The morning had passed quickly. McKenzie had flown back to Arizona, and Jake's briefing with the task force had gone well. As she left, she had tucked the profiles of the Cipriano family into her briefcase, wishing she'd had more opportunity to review them before she met with the vineyard owner, C. V. Cipriano. She was tired and anxious to get there and settle in for the night. She turned the radio on and concentrated on the beautiful scenery, determined to push thoughts of Cara from her mind. The more time and distance she could put between herself and the other woman, the better.

She turned her thoughts to something much more pleasant, the call that morning from Matt and Kalani informing her that their Syrah had won the silver medal in San Diego. Jake wished her father were alive; he would have been so proud. He had predicted that one day, as the grape matured, the wine would win a medal, but he had been murdered before he could see that prediction come true.

Jake enjoyed the cool breeze from the Pacific as she drove along the winding road. The drive to Cipriano through Santa Barbara's wine country was breathtaking, affording her a panoramic view of the ocean, steep cliffs, and rugged coastal mountains. She drove along never-ending green rolling hills covered with row upon row of grapevines as far as the eye could see.

The sun was beginning to set as she passed through the iron gates along the oak-lined road to the villa. As she exited the car and approached the carved mahogany doors, she had an odd sense of déjà vu and an even odder premonition.

Jake was directed through the villa, then an archway into a serene ramada where a natural rock waterfall flowed into a sparkling, azure pool. From there she was shown into the Cipriano study, where framed by the faint light coming in from the window a figure stood looking out at the colors of the fading sun. Jake assumed it was the vineyard owner, C. V. Cipriano. The vintner had been referred to by those initials throughout the entire task force meeting; Jake had presumed the vintner to be a man, but before her was the curved silhouette of what was obviously was a woman.

"Ms. Cipriano?" The vintner did not turn, and when she didn't get a response, Jake cleared her throat and introduced herself. "I'm Jacquelyn Biscayne from the special task force."

The odd feeling Jake had experienced since arriving at the vineyard was quickly replaced by an irritation at being so rudely ignored, and her ire began to surface.

"Look, it's been a long day. We can take this up tomorrow if this is an inconvenient time for you. Can you have someone show me to where I will be staying?" Impatience bordering on anger was evident in Jake's voice, although she tried to control it just long enough to get out of the other woman's presence.

As she turned toward the door, she muttered under her breath. "The audacity—damn it, who does she think she is? I'm here to help and all she does is bloody well ignore me." Just as she reached for the handle of the door, she heard a heart-stopping, all-too-familiar voice.

"Jake...please wait."

The voice gouged inside Jake, twisting her heart. She clenched her fists, willing the contents of her stomach to stay put. Instructing her body to turn, she found herself face to face with Cara. They stood looking at each other, neither able to speak. Poignant memories of an all-too-brief time that seemed a lifetime removed from now washed over both women.

Jake's eyes filled with tears, and that very fact made her even angrier with Cara and at herself for the double-edged emotions. Emotions spurred on by months of not knowing what had happened, compounded by the previous day's incident, surged through her.

When she had encountered Cara the previous year at Maria's Café in Nogales, she had harbored a tremendous resentment for the lawyer she deemed to be nothing less than a shark. But in the course of the ensuing investigation of the desert serial murders, Jake had gotten to know Cara the woman. And in spite of the arguing and hardheadedness that they both exhibited, she began to admire Cara on a professional level and then on a personal one. After an accident in the desert, Jake's growing warmth had escalated to an all-out attraction, which she quickly pushed aside because it hit too close to home. Feelings that she had denied for too many years began to surface when she was with Cara, and they terrified her.

Standing face to face with Cara again, now, she reeled from the onslaught of memories. Warring emotions struggled for control. Part of her wanted to hurt Cara by telling her that she no longer cared or wanted her. That she had never really loved her. Another part of her wanted to slide back into Cara's strong embrace and feel the press of moist lips against her temple as she inhaled Cara's earthy scent.

All Jake could do was to stare Cara down until the emotion overtook her and her chin began to quiver. She could feel the tears building, threatening to spill. She turned and started toward the door but stopped to regain her composure before wheeling back around, her anger winning. She let fly her indignation and a year's worth of suppressed rage over Cara's exit from her life.

"Just who in hell do you think you are?" Incensed, Jake stepped closer to Cara with each furious word. By the time she finished the sentence, she was nose to nose with Cara. "Fuck 'em and leave 'em, is that it?"

"Jake, please don't make this any harder than it already is."

"Make it harder? *Make it harder?* For who, Cara, you? 'Cause it sure as hell couldn't make it any harder for me. Let me share something with you, Counselor. This will make your day. Since you left me, there has not been a day I haven't missed or wanted you or worried where you were and if you were all right. I thought I knew hard until I saw you yesterday."

Jake felt the jealousy provoking her vengeful words. "She is very beautiful, Cara. And you share a child—fast worker!"

The closeness of Jake's body, the fire in those hazel eyes Cara missed so very much spurred her desire for the woman who had dominated her every thought, every feeling. One arm found its way around Jake's waist as her other hand caught Jake's in midair. She pulled Jake to her and covered her mouth with her own.

At first she felt the resistance as Jake pushed her away. Then the scorching heat of Jake's desire erupted and Jake's tongue accepted hers as it searched for absolution. She heard a moan as her lips left Jake's to find the pulse point on her neck, and she gently sucked the soft skin. Cara was beyond the point of rational thought as passion exploded and Jake's hands moved to her hips, pulling them closer to hers, fueling the flame. She could hear her voice repeating Jake's name over and over.

"Oh God, God, I want you." As she moved to take a nipple between her teeth through Jake's silk blouse, Jake was pulling the shirt from Cara's slacks to run her hands on the warm soft skin of Cara's back. Cara reached a hand down between them and unbuttoned Jake's jeans, then lifted her up and braced her against the door as Jake's legs wrapped around her waist.

Jake's hips jerked as Cara slid her fingers inside her clothes and across her clit. Nothing mattered except the exquisite feeling of Cara's touch. Jake's cry was hardly audible. "Please, Cara, please."

Jake moaned as Cara thrust into her. She had never experienced this kind of maddening passion and need. She felt herself nearing the edge when a knock on the door and Maggie's voice shocked them both back to reality. Jake dropped her head against Cara's neck, her breath coming in short gasps.

Cara held her close, not wanting to let her go. "I'm so sorry, oh God, baby, I am so sorry!" She lowered Jake's legs to the floor, still holding her close, then in a shaky, strained voice she spoke through the door. "Just a minute, Maggie. I'll come up to the house in a minute."

She waited until she heard footsteps leading away from the door, then pulled back to look into Jake's eyes. "Are you all right?" The slap to Cara's face echoed across the lonely months and stung her to her very core.

Jake couldn't believe what had just happened. Hearing the voice of the woman Cara was evidently involved with while she was making love to her enraged Jake. She wanted to lash out and hurt Cara.

Trembling, her voice shaking, she said, "We've had this conversation once before, if I'm remembering right. I'm here to do a job, and unfortunately we have to work together. If I had known you were C. V. Cipriano, believe me, I would not have taken this assignment."

Jake's voice steadied as she adopted an icy, professional demeanor. "Now, if you'll show me to my room, we will go over the details of this operation in the morning."

Shaken, Cara stepped back to the desk and reached for the phone. "Kate, I'm in the study with Jacquelyn Biscayne, my new assistant. Would you please come and show her to the guesthouse? And please arrange for her dinner to be served there tonight."

Cara walked toward a door on the opposite side of the room that led across another ramada toward the stables. "We'll go over what I have in the morning, after my ride with Tiana. If you need anything, let Kate know." Before Cara could retreat through the door, Jake's cold voice stopped her.

"One more thing, Counselor. Never, ever, lay your hands on me again."

CHAPTER TWELVE

Jake felt numb and was shivering in spite of the warm night. She wrapped her arms around her body as she followed the housekeeper along the lighted path to the guesthouse. The cottage sat on a bluff, secluded from the main house, overlooking the Pacific Ocean. Not even the sound of the surf beating against the craggy rocks below could drown out the roar in Jake's head. Next thing she knew she was standing in the middle of the living room, and Kate was handing her a key.

"I had your luggage put in the bedroom. The refrigerator is stocked, but if you need anything just call the main house. Ms. Cipriano requested your dinner be brought to the cottage tonight. She thought you might be tired from your trip. You're free to come and go as you wish, but you are more than welcome to join the family in the main house for meals." Kate gave Jake a warm smile. "Do you need anything, Ms. Biscayne?"

Jake stood there, frozen in place, clutching the key in her hand as Kate's voice droned on in the gray fog of her mind.

"Ms. Biscayne?"

"I'm sorry. Excuse me?"

"Might you be needing anything, Ms. Biscayne?"

"No, no, thank you. Just a good night's sleep." *And to be as far away from her—them—as I can get! Oh God, how am I going to do this?*

As soon as the housekeeper left, Jake stumbled into the bathroom, stripping off her clothes, then turned on the water as hot as she could get it. She scrubbed the scent of Cara and her passion off her body. She crawled, weary and spent, into bed, dreading the rising sun.

Jake was lying awake when the phone rang the next morning. She had been up most of the night, replaying the scene in the study with Cara. After hours of asking herself *how dare she* and berating Cara for her audacity, Jake had to admit she was just as much to blame. She had spent the rest of the night agonizing over her relationship with the enigmatic lawyer, convincing herself that she could handle her feelings and complete the assignment. What bothered her was the fact that her feelings ran the gamut, from jealousy to downright loathing to the desire she'd allowed to get out of control the previous night.

Believe me, Vittore, it will never happen again! The thought of Cara and Maggie together twisted in her stomach.

The voice on the telephone said cheerily, "Good morning, Ms. Biscayne. Ms. Cipriano requests your presence at the main house this morning for breakfast. She has asked her brothers to be there as well."

Jake instantly fumed but held her tongue. "Please tell Ms. Cipriano I will be there in half an hour." Slamming the phone down she ejected herself from the bed, grumbling under her breath the entire way. "Arrogant, irritating, impossible bitch! I should have stuck to my first impression of her high almighty self the first time I ever laid eyes on her! God damn it, just damn it all to hell."

At precisely half past the hour, Jake walked into the dining room to face—Maggie. She could feel the heat of embarrassment creeping up her neck as she wondered if Maggie had heard what was going on in the study the night before.

More important, she needed to how much Maggie knew about Cipriano and the illicit drugs, and if she knew Jake was an undercover agent. The look on Maggie's face left no doubt that she recognized Jake from the fiasco at the convention center.

Jake offered her hand, hoping Maggie would go along and not blow her cover. "I'm Jacquelyn Biscayne, Ms. Cipriano's new assistant."

Suppressing her curiosity and confusion, Maggie graciously accepted Jake's hand. "Welcome to Cipriano, Ms. Biscayne. We can certainly use your help while Maurillio recovers. Please sit. Coffee?"

Maggie was pouring two coffees when a man dressed in a light gray suit, tailored to fit, with equally expensive shoes, entered the dining room. He walked over to Maggie and kissed her on the cheek, taking one of the coffees out of her hand in the process. "Ah! Maggie, where is my charming sister? Did herself not summon us all to be in attendance this fine morning?"

He focused familiar brown eyes on Jake. "This must be the new assistant." He extended his hand to accept Jake's, then held it while his eyes leisurely roamed over her body.

"Giancarlo, you would know she takes Tiana riding every morning before breakfast if you joined us more often for breakfast. And that coffee wasn't for you."

Jake scrutinized the man who, without a doubt, was one of Cara's brothers. He was as handsome with his dark hair and eyes as Cara was beautiful.

Giancarlo entwined his arm with Jake's. "Come, let's have our coffee on the veranda while we wait for my dear sister and my brother to grace us with their presence. Tell me, dear Maggie, whose bed is my brother warming at night while you give my sister moral support?"

An angry voice interrupted before Maggie could respond. "That would be none of your business, Giancarlo."

Jake untangled her arm from Giancarlo's, turning simultaneously with Maggie to see Cara in the doorway, pushing an older, distinguished-looking gentleman in a wheelchair into the dining room.

The man's speech was slow and deliberate, but his words were clear. "Giancarlo, you will apologize to our guest. And I will never hear such insolence and disrespect for Maggie and your sister again. Is that understood?"

Giancarlo's eyes narrowed in defiance as he glared at his sister, then smiled and turned to Jake. "My apologies, madam, it was most rude of me to indicate my sister is anything but the epitome of honor and respectability." Bowing slightly to Maggie, he continued, "And to you, my dear sister-in-law, my deepest apology. Now if you all will all excuse me, I find myself late for an appointment." He walked over to his father, bent down and kissed him on the cheek, and left.

As Cara introduced her father, Jake's smile was forced and frozen on her face. She played her part, but her mind was reeling at Giancarlo's comments. *Sister-in-law—what was her brother implying? That she—Maggie, they are...? And she's married to Cara's brother?*

The anger subsided from the old man's eyes as he extended his good hand to Jake. "Welcome to our home, Miss Biscayne. You will be of great assistance to my Cara while our dear Maurillio is recovering."

Jake found her voice, avoiding Cara's eyes, which were a swirling eddy of emotion. "Thank you, sir. I shall do my best to assist Car—Ms. Vittor—Cipriano, in Maurillio's absence."

"Now, please, you will join us for breakfast."

Jake toyed with her food; so many scenarios were running through her mind. When she'd been unable to sleep the previous night, she had reviewed the files given to her at the drug task force meeting. Without a doubt, the drugs were being smuggled into Cipriano by someone who was close enough inside to get away with it for so long. Could it be one of Cara's brothers? She pondered the dynamics she had witnessed that morning, then wondered about Maggie's husband, Paolo.

She glanced up from her plate in time to see Maggie's questioning eyes on her, but when Maggie casually reached over and rubbed Cara's forearm in response to something Cara had said, Jake felt a sudden wave of overwhelming nausea. Abruptly excusing herself, she said she wanted to unpack and prepare for her meeting with Ms. Cipriano.

Jake walked along the path to the guesthouse, stopping at a gazebo to sit on a bench overlooking a bluff. She sat under a gnarled cypress tree that spread its twisted arms to provide shade from the sun. Forcing deep breaths, hoping the sick feeling in her stomach and heart would pass, she focused on the sound of the surf and the dolphins in the distance, swimming playfully around a cruise ship sailing out to sea.

I need to put her out of my mind and concentrate on why I'm here. You have a job to do. Act like a professional. It doesn't matter if she is playing house or not with her sister-in-law. She left you, remember? Jake stood up and took in a deep breath, filling her lungs with the fresh breeze off the ocean, then resolutely walked the rest of the way to the guesthouse.

CHAPTER THIRTEEN

A lone figure, clad in fatigues and a dark navy jacket, repositioned his U.S. Customs cap to shade his eyes from the glaring sun as he silently made his way through the dense stand of creosote bushes and palo verde. He paused beside a saguaro to listen to the sounds of the Sonoran Desert, his keen eye focusing on a tiny piece of fiber caught on a thorny cats-claw. The yellow-flowered bush seemed to be reaching out to the Shadow Wolf, guiding his way.

Craig Ochoa, one of the elite Indian trackers of the Tohono O'odham Reservation, had been tracking two suspected drug mules across the desert for most of the day. Stopping only to scrutinize the smallest trace or footprint that his quarry had left, he crouched, distributing his weight equally on both feet, to run his fingers, feather light, across the smooth, unmarked prints.

You can disguise your bootprint, hombre, but I will find you, and from the feel of this print and that green broken twig, you're not too far ahead. You are carrying a heavy load, my friends. Soon, you will need to rest.

It was not long before the smell of a campfire put a slight smile on the Shadow Wolf's face as he knelt and unsheathed the rifle from the scabbard on his back. He laid the rifle across the crook of his arm and reached into his pocket for a hunk of dried beef, then leaned against a rock that held the warmth of the sun. *It will be dark soon. No sense in sleeping with one eye open. You will start out at dawn, and I will be waiting.*

87

Craig watched the indigo sky darken, opening it to the vast expanse of the heavens. He began to count the myriad of stars, then smiled, knowing his brother Alejandro looked upon him as he walked the path of their ancestors. As children, growing up on the reservation, they would try to count the stars as they lay in the back of the old pickup they slept in many nights. He chuckled to himself, remembering how Alejandro always fell asleep, then in the morning would excitedly ask, "How many, how many?" *Now I ask you, my brother, how many stars lead you on your way?*

Craig had worked every day for over a year since the man he had regarded as a friend had senselessly murdered his brother. Persevering each day, tirelessly tracking the drug runners in hopes of finding a link to Sandro, he had many times gotten close, only to see the serpent's shadow disappear, vaporizing into thin air. Craig wasn't alone in his search. His friend, Matt Peyson of the U.S. Border Patrol and Alejandro's boss, searched too. Sandro's evil had defiled and stained the desert with the blood of the innocent. Craig had no doubt that the land of his ancestors would seek and take its revenge.

Taking down the two drug runners went without a problem. Craig silently walked right into their camp just before dawn, bent over the smoldering campfire, poured himself a cup of stale coffee, sat, and waited until the two men woke a short while later. Afterward, he sat, relaxed, waiting for the border patrol helicopter to transport him, the two runners, and their load of marijuana and fifty kilos of cocaine back to Nogales.

Kalani ran a comparison of a sample of the cocaine Craig brought in against a sample from a recent bust from the Rivera cartel while Matt anxiously hovered next to her. The Drug Enforcement Administration and U.S. Customs Service task force, Operation Monsoon Rain, was systematically narrowing down the transportation routes the cartel and Sandro used to transport the drugs and illegal contraband across the border into the United States. Their methods varied from the simplicity of the two traffickers on foot that Craig had brought in to modern modes of transportation, including high-speed boats and private jets.

Kalani teased, "Matt, if you would give me room to move here, I could get this done a lot faster."

Matt put his arms around her waist and pulled her close. He liked the feel of Kalani, the smell of her hair, the way she smiled. She was a woman who could hold her own. And did, raising their daughter Teresa by herself as she had.

"You know, we have to tell Teresa I'm her father one day soon."

Kalani buried her face into his muscular shoulder. *Matt, I love you. I have since we were kids, but the only person you could ever see was Jake. Are you over her? You say you want us to be a family and raise our daughter together. Can I trust that? Can Teresa? What if Jake—no, Jake wouldn't. But what about you, Matt? What about love? You haven't once said you love me.*

"I know, Matt, and we will. I just need more time to prepare her. She has known you all her life—but as a friend, not as her father. Please be patient, Matt. I...I just need a bit more time."

"Hey, how about I pick you up after you're done here and the three of us go to dinner?"

Before Kalani could answer, Matt's cell rang. He looked at the caller ID and pressed the talk button. "Jake, I was getting a mite worried about you, haven't heard from you."

Matt listened to what Jake was saying, then his voice hardened, his blue eyes flashing his anger. "What! Damn it, Jake, when you found out who it was, why didn't you ask them to replace you on the team?"

Matt was hollering, unmindful of Kalani looking at him questioningly, wondering what was going on. "Get yourself out of there now, Jake, you can't be effective working that close to her." He listened a few seconds, then growled, "Give me a few minutes to get to my office."

Distracted, he absently glanced toward Kalani. "Jake will call you later," he said, and was gone.

Kalani shook her head and went back to her work. "Well, so much for dinner."

Matt tried to get a hold on his anger as he hurriedly walked toward his office. *Vittore! You've hurt her enough. Damn it, this time you could get her killed!* Matt had accepted it when Jake fell in love with Cara and chose her over him. He even liked the pertinacious attorney. She was a perfect match for the headstrong doctor. They were like two colliding stars when they met, neither giving an inch, but they lit up the heavens. It was a battle of wills, which they both lost when they fell in love with each other. He had watched Jake withdraw from living after Sam and her father were killed—and again when Vittore walked out on her. He wasn't about to stand by and let it happen again.

They were both working on the same case. Matt was part of Operation Monsoon Rain. Its directive: to follow the drug trail from Mexico into the U.S. Both had the same agenda, and that was to find Sandro. Both knew the trail would eventually lead to the man who had betrayed them. After Mexico, the pieces finally fit; it had been there staring him right in the face all along.

Matt had gone over files and notes from the Gulf War and the unsolved murders he investigated during that time. Kalani had sent the DNA evidence they had on the serial killings in the desert to Washington for comparison with the DNA evidence from the brutal, savage killings in Kuwait and Iraq. They came up with an unquestionable match. Sandro had been killing as far back as 1991.

It dawned on Matt, after he faxed the information Jake requested, that he had run out of Kalani's office without an explanation. He looked at his watch and groaned. *Way to go, Matt. She's already picked Teresa up, and they are probably home by now.*

CHAPTER FOURTEEN

As the week passed, Jake went about quietly establishing herself into the routine at Cipriano. Cara had given her an office, opposite her own, in the sales and tasting room. Jake had begun by reading the personal files and sorting through the work visas. She reviewed the financial reports of every member of the family, including Cara and Maggie. Both women were independently wealthy. Cara had a trust, as did her two brothers, established by their parents before they died in an auto accident when Cara was three. Being a successful attorney, Cara would have been wealthy without the trust, which had grown substantially over the years due to the success of the vineyard.

The source and magnitude of Maggie's wealth, as well as the discovery that Maggie was the only daughter of Armanno Santini, of the neighboring vineyard and the internationally known Santini Imports, surprised Jake. The marriage of Maggie and Paolo had merged the two most prestigious vineyards in Southern California. Jake's mind reeled at the implications. She had yet to meet Maggie's husband, Paolo, or her brother Robert, who managed and lived at Santini Vineyards and who also was overseer of Santini Imports. She was curious and made a mental note to ask Cara about it in the morning.

Without drawing too much attention or suspicion to herself, Jake always kept an eye on the aging room and the wine barrels with the false bottoms. The drugs Cara had found had been moved, tracked by the task force to a warehouse in Albuquerque,

New Mexico, before being distributed to other locations throughout the country. The task force could close down this single route for trafficking but still not be able to touch the cartel or its leaders.

Jake had taken to eating her meals in the cottage and spending what little time she wasn't working sitting on a bench in the gazebo overlooking the bluff, watching the breakers crest against the shoreline. She worked as hard as the rest, from dawn to sunset, welcoming the exhaustion when she finally crawled into bed at night. All the time spent worrying and missing Cara, wondering where she was and if she was all right, had been torment. It had taken her many months to realize that Cara had just walked, just left her without a word or a good-bye. But being so close to her every day, knowing she was going home at night to a family, to Maggie, was a different kind of torment.

Her thoughts went to McKenzie and the night in San Diego they had made love. She felt guilty about not calling the fiery redhead. *It wasn't the same, but McKenzie is a wonderful lover. She's passionate and desirable and could make any woman's heart beat faster. Besides, she's beautiful, smart, and fun to be with. I never thought I could respond to another woman, not after Cara. I had never been with a woman before her, and I loved her more than I ever thought it was possible to love anyone.*

Who are you trying to convince, Jake? Be honest with yourself. When Cara touched and loved you, nothing else mattered; you could never get enough of her. Even now, you can't stop yourself from looking at her when she is unaware—and remembering. Watching her with Maggie drives you crazy. Christ, get over it, Jake. Jake cursed Cara into the empty darkness. She rolled over and punched her pillow, trying to drive the thoughts and images of her brown-eyed nemesis from her mind.

Jake was restless. She had been tossing and turning for the past two hours trying to get to sleep. She got up, deciding to walk down to the beach, and threw on a pair of jeans and a T-shirt, then started down the road to the trail. It was a beautiful night, and the trail was well lighted from the rising full moon. A balmy breeze off the ocean felt good and eased her thoughts as she walked along the path. She made it down the winding trail, then slipped her shoes off and walked barefoot along the ocean's edge, allowing the cool sand and gentle surf to run between her toes.

After climbing back up the trail, Jake stopped at the gazebo to sit and rest a bit and to look out across the water at the moon where it rested upon the edge of the ocean, cascading ripples of light across the gentle waves to the shoreline. She was about to head back to the cottage when a sound made her turn toward the main house.

What was that? An animal? No, it sounded like a—a baby crying. On several nights she thought she'd heard a similar sound but had attributed it to one of the many birds fishing along the beach. She walked a bit closer to the main house and stopped dead in her tracks as she looked up to the balcony of Cara's bedroom.

Cara was standing behind Maggie in a robe that was half-open, and Maggie, who was dressed in a skimpy nightgown, was holding a baby over her shoulder. Jake felt her knees go weak as she watched Cara put her arm around Maggie's shoulders. The look on Maggie's face said it all. *She's in love with Cara!*

Jake backed up, stumbling, not wanting to see any more. As soon as she was far enough down the road and out of sight of the house, she dropped to her knees in the middle of the road and sobbed, her arms wrapped around her body. "Damn you to hell, Cara Vittore! Damn you to hell!"

Jake didn't remember how she made it back to the cottage or how she managed to crawl into bed, but she did remember the unbearable pain and the loathing she now held for the *padrone* of Cipriano. She looked into the bathroom mirror at her red, puffy eyes and vowed Cara Vittore would never again get to her. Not in this lifetime. *It's time to toughen up, Jake. You once believed there was a basic genetic difference between her and the rest of the human race. How right you were!*

She walked back into the bedroom, picked up her phone, and dialed McKenzie's number.

Cara was dragging. Baby Stephen had been up for the last week with colic, and sleep was just a faint memory. She had fallen asleep the previous night with the baby still at her breast and wasn't aware he'd spit up until Maggie gently lifted him from her arms. Maggie always seemed to know when Stephen was fussy or when she needed help. She got out of bed many nights without waking Cara to cradle and feed him with the breast milk Cara expressed and bottled in case she wasn't there during the day.

Cara leaned against the sink looking into the bathroom mirror at the dark circles under her eyes. *God, this past year has been brutal, and it hasn't been any easier since I've been back at Cipriano. I don't know what I would do without Maggie. I need to do something nice for her; take her out to dinner or something. Tiana will be in school most of the day soon, and Maggie needs to get out and make a life for herself.*

She was wiping the haze off the mirror after her shower when her thoughts turned to Jake and the way she'd looked as Cara had watched her, unseen, the day before.

Cara had ridden Ebony out in the early morning to look over a section of land she was considering planting. The cool ocean breeze and solitude always helped her to think and to clear away the troubles for a while. She sat on a knoll under a grove of oak trees looking to the valley below, nestled between the Santa Ynez and San Rafael coastal range. The rolling hills were shrouded in a low, hugging fog. She watched a rider galloping, appearing then vanishing in and out of the mist.

She knew instinctively it was Jake riding Eldorado, her prize golden palomino. It was breathtaking to watch rider and horse moving together as one through the mist. Jake's strong body sat the horse proudly, much as a lover, gently guiding, encouraging, and anticipating. Cara's heart began to race as she watched Jake slide her hands down the horse's mane, gently showing her praise to the powerful animal. Her mind had no choice but to replay the image of Jake's face in the candlelight as she lay beneath her, running her fingers lovingly along her back, pulling her hips closer as they lay naked together, loving each other. Cara remembered every time, every sound, each whimper.

A shiver of need surged through her, her body remembering the way they responded to each other's touch. The look on Jake's face when she reached her climax never failed to excite Cara beyond her own pleasure. *Oh Jake, how could I have told you about the rape in Mexico and the ambiguous results of the HIV test? How could I tell you about the pregnancy and my agony deciding whether to have an abortion? I could never have lived with your pity or look of disgust or fear if I touched you. I just couldn't take the chance, my love, and now it is too late. You hate me more now than you did that day on the witness stand or in Maria's Café. It is so hard to see you every day, to be so close I could reach out and touch you, and to know I never will again.*

CHAPTER FIFTEEN

J ake adjusted the last surveillance camera in the decorative wooden cork on top of the exquisite, hand-carved wine barrel adorning the entrance to the aging room. The embellishment had been easy enough to duplicate to accommodate the pinpoint-size camera. The position of the sculpted barrel was strategically perfect so that the camera would record anyone or anything that went in and out of the aging room and the area where the recyclable barrels were kept.

Jake's fingers eased over the sculptured wood of the barrel that depicted a young Cara riding a black stallion rearing back on his hind legs. Her wild dark hair was blown by an unseen wind, her piercing eyes were challenging. She remembered that look; the artist had caught it well.

The last time Jake saw it was a year ago, just before Cara had been swept away by a flash flood. Cara had risked her life that day trying to save an immigrant family. Jake would never forget the look on Cara's face, just before she and her horse were swept away, as she crested the arroyo and twisted in her saddle to look back seconds before the raging water hit full force. Their eyes locked for a moment before Cara disappeared into the inky torrent of black water. In that moment, Cara's intense brown eyes penetrated Jake's with a ragged strength that bared her soul, challenging and defying death.

Jake had felt an infinite loss even before she dismounted and stumbled along the arroyo in the dark, searching frantically for any sign of the other woman, knowing there wasn't a chance in hell that she could have survived. Yet, when Jake had walked into the ranger station the following morning, there Cara was—caked in mud, bruised, and bleeding, but alive.

Jake was staring at the beautiful piece of art, lost in the memory, when a voice boomed across the room from the bar.

"What is it you find most interesting, the workmanship of the carving or the master of Cipriano?"

Startled, Jake turned to face a man standing several feet behind her at the tasting bar, pouring himself a drink.

"Tell me, which one of her women are you? Don't tell me she has grown tired of my wife already?"

The man had obviously been drinking and had a wild look about him. He was bigger than Giancarlo, but he had the same finely chiseled features. Jake quickly deduced that he had to be Paolo, Maggie's husband. He looked disheveled, as if he had slept in his clothes. His hair was tousled and his face wore several days' stubble. The familiar brown eyes were hard and cold.

Jake started to say something when a harsh voice interrupted.

"You will show respect and watch your mouth, Paolo, or you will not be allowed to stay at Cipriano. You are only here because of Grandfather, but if he knew..."

Cara was seething with anger. What she didn't say was if Grandfather found out about the abuse to Maggie and Tiana, Paolo would be disinherited and exiled from Cipriano. Sebastian Cipriano was old-country Italy and believed it a disgrace to raise a hand to a woman or a child. He had taught Cara and both of her brothers the respect of his beliefs and ways and the honor of the Cipriano family name.

Sister and brother faced off, glaring at each other, the hatred evident in their eyes. The tension between the two was palpable. Jake fixed her eyes on Cara. She could see Cara's jaw clenching and her hands shaking. And for the first time since she had arrived at Cipriano, she became aware of the dark circles rimming Cara's eyes, her tiredness and weight loss.

Walking between the two, Jake decided it was time to intercede and defuse the situation. She turned toward Paolo. "I'm Jacquelyn Biscayne, Ms. Cipriano's new assistant."

Not waiting for a response, she quickly turned toward Cara. "I have several items to go over with you before the festivities tomorrow night. Do you have a few minutes?"

The brief distraction was all Cara needed to regain her composure. "Certainly, and I apologize for my brother's behavior. Please, we can go to my office."

Cara leveled her eyes on her brother. "Your things have been moved to the guest rooms on the first floor. You are not welcome on the second floor, Paolo. I warn you—stay away from them both."

Cara turned to follow Jake to her office, then stopped without turning around. "I have filed divorce papers for her, Paolo; you will be served sometime this week."

Paolo's voice was acrid with sarcasm as his spiteful, bloodshot eyes burned into his sister's back. "Of course, sister, no easier way to have my wife all to yourself, now, is there? Wasn't it enough blood for you that Stephen had to die because of your lust for Maggie?"

Cara's face drained of color, and Jake thought she was going to faint as her step faltered. Without a second's hesitation, Jake stepped to Cara's side. Leaning into her to support her, she spoke quietly. "Now is not the time for this, Cara, let it go. We cannot jeopardize this operation. Too much is at stake."

Cara gave Jake a shaky nod and followed her into her office. She stood rigidly at the window behind her desk, the muscles in her jaw clenched tight and her shoulders set, looking out but seeing nothing. Paolo's words had gnawed at her soul and left it bleeding, opening up a floodgate of pain and regret. *Dear God, I know I was responsible the day Stephen died.*

Her younger brother enthusiastically burst into her room the morning of his wedding to Maggie and found her and Maggie in bed together. Maggie had come to Cipriano before dawn that morning and entered through the kitchen door, as she had so many mornings before when they were growing up. She'd slid under the covers and put her arm around Cara's waist, laying her head on her shoulder. Even in her sleep, Cara knew it was Maggie. As she breathed in Maggie's familiar scent, her arms instinctively went around the warm body as they had so many times before when Maggie would sleep over when they were kids.

She woke with a start when her brain realized it had never had the sensation of Maggie's scent in a dream before. "Maggie, what are you doing, you can't be here!" She tried to pull out of Maggie's arms.

Maggie held on tighter. Cara could feel Maggie's tears on her shoulder as she whispered, "I know, but I had to come, Cara. You have avoided me for years. Every time you came home and wouldn't see me, it tore my heart out. I missed you, I miss my best friend."

"God, don't you know how much I miss you too." Cara's tears fell as she held on to Maggie. "I wanted so much to call you, to see you."

Maggie lifted up, her blue eyes filled with moisture. "Why, why didn't you? I waited so long. Best friends are supposed to be just that, best friends."

Cara sobbed as she pulled Maggie into an embrace. "Oh, Maggie, I couldn't after we—Stephen has always loved you. Grandfather, your father—it never would have been accepted."

"That doesn't excuse you, Cara Vittore."

Cara held Maggie, both knowing it could never be. Maggie was marrying Stephen that day. After they both had cried as much as they could, they just lay in each other's arms.

Maggie hiccupped and said, "You know I had a bridesmaid's dress made for you, don't you?"

Cara looked at her in disbelief. "You didn't."

"Yes, and in your favorite color, too."

"Well, then, I guess we better get up and get you married to my brother, don't you think?"

"Yeah, I think."

Maggie gave Cara a last hug and kissed her on the lips. It was at that moment Stephen excitedly burst into Cara's room with his tie in his hand.

The look of hurt and disbelief on his face was forever burned into every fiber of Cara's being. Stephen had died that day thinking his sister and the woman he loved had betrayed him.

CHAPTER SIXTEEN

Jake thought she had resolved her feelings for Cara after seeing her with Maggie on the veranda, but Paolo's words taunted her. The images of Cara and Maggie that invaded her mind evoked an ache she couldn't deal with. In spite of her pain, she wanted to go to Cara and take her into her arms to soothe Cara's grief. Instead, Jake's voice was tight and edgy. "You wanted to go over the final preparations before the festivities tomorrow?"

Cara straightened her shoulders and took in a ragged breath as if she had forgotten Jake was in the room. Jake hardly recognized the angst-ridden voice that answered her. "Can we go over this later this morning, please? Now is not a good time. I have something I need to tend to."

Jake struggled to control her emotions, concentrating on the assignment and the reason she was there. "I swept this room and placed the camera. I have a meeting with Josh McNeil this morning in town. As far as anyone is concerned, I'm going into town on a last-minute errand for the open house tomorrow. Mrs. Cipriano—Maggie—and Hattie seemed to have everything well organized."

Cara nodded and Jake turned to leave, then stopped. She steadied her voice, trying to conceal her emotion. "I invited a guest to come to stay a few days. I hope that's all right?"

Cara turned and looked at Jake with questioning eyes. "Of course it is, Jake, you don't need to ask. I'll have Kate prepare a room. Will they be staying at the main house?"

Jake swallowed the lump in her throat as she looked directly into Cara's tormented eyes. "Thank you, but no, McKenzie will stay at the guesthouse with me."

Cara simply turned to stare out the window as Jake quietly left her office.

McKenzie hadn't expected it but was elated to get Jake's call inviting her to come to Cipriano for the Vintners' Association Festival, at which Cipriano had an annual open house, with many of the local artists displaying their work and a special invitation dinner and dance after. Jake didn't say much over the phone, just that she would explain when she saw her. McKenzie was anxious to see Jake and rescheduled all her appointments so she could leave early.

She was passing by Tehachapi and the cutoff to Palm Springs when she pulled over to watch the wind turbines spinning. She thought how similar the winds of fate were, catching one's life and twisting it in different directions. And about Cara and how she'd loved her from the moment she laid eyes on the freshman law student in her father's pub, when Cara had come in to interview for a job. The tall, brown-eyed brunette, with her olive skin, was beyond doubt the most attractive woman McKenzie had the pleasure to ever lay her Irish eyes on. When Cara sat on a stool in the middle of the stage and began to strum her guitar and sing, McKenzie knew they would be lovers.

Cara was finally going meet up with her mentor; they had been missing each other most of the week, leaving notes. They finally agreed to meet at the Keltic Knot. It was Saturday night and Cara was anxious. She had been busy settling in, running to classes and working, and hadn't spent much time getting to know McKenzie since she'd started working at her father's pub. But she explained that her hotshot mentor was going to stop by and then asked if McKenzie would show her to the table she had set up close to the small stage.

After her first set of the night, Cara rushed back to the kitchen to help serve and wait tables during the break. McKenzie was stuffing the boxties and asked the taller woman to reach something for her from the top of a self. Her eyes traveled down Cara's backside while the smirk on her face warned of a bit of fun at Cara's expense. Then, emphasizing the wonderful Irish lilt that seemed to come out more when she was up to mischief, she asked, "Have you seen that high-and-mighty mentor of yours yet, love? I don't remember ya tellin' me her name."

Cara stopped and thought for a minute, then her face turned red. "She left a message on my cell phone, but not a phone number. McKenzie, I never even got her name! I never asked. The list was up but I was too busy to look at it, and when I found her note on the message board, I don't remember seeing a name. We kept missing each other all week until the last note told me to meet her here tonight. God, how stupid can I get! McKenzie, please, when she shows up, get her name so I don't look like a complete idiot!"

Laughing, McKenzie teased, "Well, now, she's that good, is she? Are we putting on the dog a bit? And just how might ya be knowing it's a woman?"

"Well, the voice sounded like a woman's, and a student in one of my classes was complaining and saying he hoped to get the one I got and that she was quite the—well, uh..." Cara's face flamed red.

McKenzie erupted in laughter.

"Come on, Kenzie, this is the, and I emphasize, the *most sought-after law student, and for some reason she has agreed to mentor me. I can learn a lot from her."*

McKenzie's green eyes sparkled, then sobered a bit. "Hmm, Cara Vittore. Of that, I am quite sure."

After the pub had closed, Cara helped McKenzie clean up for the night. "You don't think I missed her? Or do you think she just didn't show up?"

"What difference does it make? You'll catch up with each other eventually."

Cara sulked. "I was supposed to turn in a plan Monday morning that my mentor had to approve. It's Saturday, McKenzie, and I have no idea how to get in touch with her."

McKenzie finishing picking up the glasses from the tables. "Quit your fussing, everything will turn out as it should."

Irritated, Cara said, "You just wouldn't understand, McKenzie."

McKenzie's green eyes flashed. "Oh, you don't say now, and just why might that be, Cara Vittore? Because my lot in life is mopping up floors?" Maggie turned and walked toward the office to give her father the detail from the register. "I think it's time for you to be sayin' good night, Cara Vittore, and lock the door on your way out, please."

The next morning, Cara stood in the doorway of the pub with a rose in her hand and a sheepish look on her face, watching McKenzie set the bar up for the day.

"What's the matter, Yank?"

"Why didn't you tell me who you were? I made such an ass of myself."

"I'm still the same person, Cara." McKenzie smiled mischievously. "Guess ya thought I was only good for pulling pints, mopping up, and serving drunks, now, didn't ya?" she teased as she walked around the bar, setting the chairs down on the freshly mopped floor. "My grandmother always said, 'Don't be judging a book by its cover, Kenzie girl, looks and impressions can be deceiving'. She was a firm believer that every person had their worth no matter what their station in life."

Cara's mouth still hung open even as McKenzie's eyes twinkled above her broad, cat-ate-the-mouse grin. "Besides, we all need shakin' up a bit now and then—don't we? Better close that mouth of yours or you'll be a-catchin' flies."

Cara finally spoke. "Hey, you didn't sound like that over the phone. Say, didn't they tell me you spoke several languages?"

McKenzie laughed with delight. "That's right, Yank."

McKenzie looked at her watch and realized she had been reminiscing. She wanted to get to Santa Barbara; her thoughts were on Jake and the odd way her voice sounded on the phone when she had called to invite her to come for the festival. *I want you to be mine, Jake, and I will do everything I can to make that happen.*

CHAPTER SEVENTEEN

The stench of decaying flesh and the metallic smell of dried blood assaulted the craggy detective's senses, making his eyes water and his nostrils flare as he grimaced and examined the remains of what was once a living being. The atrocities one human could render upon another never failed to sicken and enrage him.

"Jesus Christ, Hank, what kind of fucking animals would do a thing like this? She couldn't have been more than sixteen or seventeen."

The flashing lights from the squad car illuminated the hardcore homicide detective's scrubby face with an eerie, intermittent light. He had seen every imaginable heinous crime in the book, or so he'd thought.

"These three were shot execution style, Harry. Hands bound behind their backs, tied to their ankles." The small Oriental medical examiner stood in his stocking feet several feet away. Han-Kiong cautiously paced backward, placing his feet inside his own tracks.

"Looks like someone was trying to send a message." Harry chewed on an unlit cigar as he crouched down to examine the wounds on one of the bodies.

"Message, my ass. Whoever did the butchery here did it for the pure pleasure of it. The cuts were methodic and deliberate, intended to inflict pain, but not death. They were probably kept alive for most of the fun."

Harry was careful to step within the pathway Han-Kiong had already processed and marked so as not to contaminate possible evidence. He stood over the decomposed bodies of three men that lay face down in their own dried blood, their brains mingled and scattered across the blood-soaked ground.

He watched as Han-Kiong placed what was left of the eyelids of one of the victims into a bottle, saying, "Sadistic sons-a-bitches made 'em watch the torture on the girl before they put them out of their misery."

Harry used his pen to push back the shredded remains of the shirt that was embedded in the torn flesh of one of the dead men's back. "What's your take on this, Hank? Looks to me like—"

"And you'd be right, Harry. Someone who knew how to inflict deadly torture with a whip mutilated them pretty damn good. These three had to be in agony and near death before they were finished off with a bullet to the back of the head."

The medical examiner pushed his wire-rimmed glasses back up on his nose with the back of his gloved wrist. "By the time they were shot, they were probably begging for the bullet."

Harry looked down at the exposed naked body of the unrecognizable female form. "The girl, was she raped?"

"Looks like it, Harry. Hard to tell, as mutilated as she is, and with the state of decomposition—it's just hard to say right now. I'll have a preliminary as soon as I can, maybe tomorrow if I can get some help. And if the good citizens of Los Angeles would give my office a break and do something else for recreation instead of murder."

Han-Kiong bagged several severed fingers as he looked around the abandoned warehouse district, knowing he had his work cut out for him. "Who found them? This place has been deserted for years."

"A night watchman called it in. He checks on the place every so often. Says he hasn't been here in over a week. How long do you think they've been here, Hank?"

"Three, could be four days."

Something was skulking at the back of Harry's mind. "Are all the victims Hispanic?"

"It's kind of hard to tell in the dark with their faces blown off the way they are, but I would say yes, the girl definitely."

"Any ID on them?"

The slight Oriental man looked over the top of his glasses. "Nothing yet, Harry. And if you let me work here instead of guessing at answers to your questions, I will have confirmed answers for you sooner."

Flashes of similar murder scenes began to fire through Harry's mind like a slide show as he looked down at the girl. Some he had seen when he served in Iraq, and some in photographs when he'd visited a friend in law enforcement in Nogales, Arizona, a little over a year ago.

Harry turned pale when the kaleidoscope of pictures finally merged. "I'll be damned. I'll just be damned! He's surfaced!"

Han-Kiong's eyes followed the detective's retreating form, his question barely penetrating the distraction of the normally stoic detective. "Who's surfaced, Harry?"

Harry yelled back over his shoulder as he hurried toward his car. "Evil personified, Hank. The Serpent himself has risen!"

Harry stood in his office staring at a picture of a military unit, his eyes focused on Captain Matt Peyson and the handsome olive complexion of the smiling face of the man standing to his right. Harry was the commanding officer of the Special Forces unit Matt and Sandro had been assigned to in Iraq. They were cousins, both raised by Matt's mother in Arizona. Matt thought of Sandro as a brother, but they were as different as night and day. Matt played everything by the book, while Sandro bent the rules, but each watched the other's back and both made it through Desert Storm and home.

While in Iraq, Harry had assigned Matt as the investigating officer in a series of unsolved rapes and mutilation murders in Kuwait. It was a time of war, of lawless confusion and untold atrocities against humanity. The murders remained unsolved until Matt had connected Sandro to the murders after Sandro was exposed as both the drug lord, *El Serpiente*, and as the Nogales pipeline murderer in Arizona.

Harry had seen the look in Matt's eyes exposing his inner turmoil. He saw the pain of failure and the hurt of betrayal. Matt had dealt with the underbelly of society—had seen the apocalypse of war, and survived. Through it all, he remained steadfast, a simple man with solid beliefs. No one could ever beat down Matt Peyson—no one but himself. He blamed himself for Sandro's reign of savageness and murder because he hadn't seen what had been right in front of him all along. Harry knew the day would come when Matt would face off with the devil. He only hoped that Matt would not walk through the portal of hell and sacrifice his soul.

Reluctantly he picked up the phone and dialed. "Matt, it's Harry."

Josh McNeil lowered the file he had been reading and looked across his desk at Jake. "Everything points to one, if not both, of the Cipriano brothers being involved here, Jake. The extent and amount of cocaine filtering through Cipriano Vineyards would be impossible otherwise." He thoughtfully eyed the document again. "If I had to make a guess, though, I'd put my money on the older one. Paolo."

"Tell me, what is your reasoning for that, Josh?" Jake went on, "Giancarlo lives well and likes the finer things in life, including a home in Montecito, which cost him a small fortune, where he has a collection of very expensive cars." Jake looked up from the report she was reading. "From what I've read, it appears he not only has expensive taste in cars but women as well."

McNeil agreed with a raise of an eyebrow, turned a few pages of the report in his hands, then played the role of devil's advocate. "And he makes enough to pay for all of that, Jake. In addition to handling the Cipriano and Santini legal affairs, he has a huge trust he can dip into. We've gone over his financial records with a fine-tooth comb, and there isn't a decimal point out of place. As for Paolo, he has had an axe to grind with his grandfather and his sister for years, even more so now."

Jake focused her attention fully on what he was saying. "Now? Something I don't know?"

McNeil quickly considered what and how much to say. "I do not disregard any implication or rumor, Jake. Everything, no matter how seemingly insignificant, is checked out to see if there is a possible connection or lead. As far as Paulo, he has held a long-standing vendetta against his grandfather and his sister."

Confusion crossed Jake's face. "Long-standing?"

"He is the elder son, and in the Italian way and tradition, he should have been named successor when Sebastian Cipriano stepped down some years back. Seems Sebastian broke with tradition and chose his granddaughter Cara to take his place when she was still a young girl. And it's not that she wasn't the best choice. Her reputation as an attorney and her success in business are stellar, and she's made friends in high places. In fact, we were able to zero in on Cipriano Vineyards as the drug connection in Santa Barbara because she called one of those friends in the attorney general's office with her suspicions."

McNeil hesitated, but Jake sensed there was more. "What's the rest, Josh?"

He squared himself across from Jake and looked her in the eye. "Cara came back to the States from Europe when her grandfather had a stroke."

"Europe?"

"Yes, Italy specifically. That's where she went after she...uh, left Arizona," he cleared his throat, "after the incident in Mexico." McNeil paused to allow Jake time to process what he was saying. From the look of surprise on her face, he realized she might not know the whole story, and if she didn't, he was unsure how much he should tell her. He knew withholding certain information from Jake could be dangerous, in more ways than one, so he continued.

"She is also representing Paolo's wife in a divorce. Magdalene Santini was Stephen Cipriano's fiancée. She was pregnant. But Stephen was killed in an auto accident the day they were to be married. And since a union was predestined between the two families, Paolo and Magdalene were married. He was a chaser before they were married and that didn't change after the wedding. He's a mean drunk and is known to beat on the women he picks up. Now that Cara Cipriano has returned, it seems Mrs. Cipriano has found the courage to leave the SOB. Rumor has it Cara and her sister-in-law are involved."

Jake couldn't help the twinge of jealousy nor the anger that edged around the corners of her hazel eyes. As hard as she tried to toughen her reaction, it stung her to think she had been just a passing distraction.

McNeil noticed the barely detectable reflexive flinch and slight tightening of Jake's jaw. "You all right with this?"

Jake could see it on his face; he was skirting around the question he had to ask. And true to her nature, she faced it head on. "Did you know about Vittore and me when you chose me for this assignment?"

McNeil respected Jake and didn't have a homophobic bone in his body, and he knew Jake deserved an honest answer. "I knew you worked together in Arizona and then on a sensitive covert operation in Mexico, but until right now I wasn't sure you were anything other than friends."

Jacquelyn Lee Biscayne was a proud woman, and she wasn't ashamed of her relationship with Cara. Her hazel eyes frosted over as she fixed them on McNeil's face. "Does it make a difference?"

McNeil was quick to answer. "Only if it interferes with your judgment or compromises this operation in any way, Jake. So you tell me. Does it?"

Jake had asked herself that very question many times since her path had again crossed Cara's. Undeniably, Cara had run a stake through her heart, but Jake was powerless to prevent the breath that caught in her chest as she'd watched the splendor of the olive-skinned woman riding amongst the grapevines. Her grace and beauty were more inspiring than the indescribable sunset painted with hues of burnt orange and golden yellow.

Jake's voice was even, convincing, and void of emotion. "No. My history with Cara Vittore is just that, history. It does not and will not jeopardize this operation."

McNeil thought he'd seen a hint of doubt in Jake's armor, but he accepted her word and hoped he was not making a mistake.

CHAPTER EIGHTEEN

The additional help hired to set up for the open house and the Vintners' Association Festival were busy putting the final decorative touches to the vineyards. The brass bar railing and lanterns in the tasting room all had been buffed to a warm glow, and the hardwood floor reflected the pride of Cipriano and the occasion. The mood was undeniably festive, and light conversation and laughter echoed through the cavernous aging rooms as workers eagerly dusted oak barrels and shiny stainless steel pipes and tanks. Mouth-watering aromas coming from Hattie's kitchen wafted throughout the vineyards.

Tiana loved festival time even more than Christmas—except for the presents, of course. The staff lovingly looked out for the little tomboy as she excitedly ran from one place to another in her excitement and fear that she was going to miss out on some wonderful happening or not be present to direct or add her opinion. After an early dinner, Hattie chased her off the polished banisters in the main house, but not before being driven to total distraction when Tiana slid down them for the umpteenth time. Armed with a handful of chocolate chip cookies, Tiana stood in the middle of the tasting room, mischievously eyeing the freshly waxed hardwood floors.

After her meeting with McNeil and its revelations about Cara and Maggie, Jake had needed to steady her emotions before driving back to Cipriano. She had scolded herself repeatedly for allowing her heart to be so vulnerable, so affected by Cara Vittore's past and by everything she had seen of her relationship with her sister-in-law. McNeil was taking a risk letting her stay on this case. She was undercover in a dangerous situation that could be deadly if she could not isolate her personal feelings.

She'd decided to take a walk along Butterfly Beach after stopping at a coffee shop in Montecito that offered, along with a superb latte, an undisturbed view of the Channel Islands off the coast. After an easy walk down a street of quaint and unique specialty shops, Jake had made her way along a canopied, foliage-lined dirt path until it opened to an expanse where clear cloudless blue sky met with sapphire blue ocean. She'd rolled up her pants legs, removed her shoes and socks, then walked along the edge of the surf, allowing her feet to sink into the wet sand and letting the cool water caress her bare legs.

The rhythmic pounding of the waves and the cleansing ocean breeze challenged her with a myriad of questions. A movement of color against the endless blue caught Jake's eye, and she focused on the poetic, graceful skill of a paraglider soaring effortlessly on the current as if guided by invisible strings. She had envied the simplicity and freedom the silent, lone figure symbolized as she'd turned toward the mocking sound of a strutting western gull, comical in its way, denouncing the validity of the intruder in its space. Jake had shaken her head slightly, smiling at the scene. *Well, we all have our problems, it seems.* She'd sat a while longer on a piece of driftwood, absorbing the sun and the welcomed tranquility, listening to the waves breaking on the shore.

Having returned to Cipriano, Jake was going over the videotapes of the day's activity when she heard a loud crashing noise coming from the tasting room. Knowing the workers had finished and left almost an hour earlier, she quickly switched on the monitor to the hidden cameras. McNeil's sources indicated something big, possibly a large shipment of cocaine, would be entering the Santa Barbara area during the Vintners' Festival. McNeil had planted two agents in the crew, but they had reported in earlier that they were leaving for the night—although she knew they would be close by if she needed backup.

Seeing no movement on the monitors, Jake retrieved the pistol she kept hidden and locked in her desk drawer, then quietly, in the shadows cast by the dim light coming from the tasting room, inched her way along the wall toward the source of the noise. She reached the end of the hallway, pausing a moment to listen, and was about to enter the room when a hand gripped the wrist of her gun hand and another one pressed across her mouth. She felt herself being pulled back into a warm body.

Jake had chambered a round, and her finger pressed against the trigger. She was about to twist the gun toward whoever was holding her captive when a familiar voice whispered into her ear.

"Shh, quiet. I heard it too. If it's someone planting the drugs, we'll be able to find out who it is. Let's not spook 'em."

Cara's lips and breath were against her ear, and Jake could feel her warm, full breasts pressed tight against her back. Her heart rate increased. Her stomach clenched. An involuntary shiver ran through her. She mentally chastised herself. *Good Lord, Jake! This is no time to be feeling or thinking what you are right now. This woman has got you crazy!*

Cara likewise felt a jolt of electricity surge through her body as she pressed against Jake. She loved the smell of Jake's hair, and she couldn't help the unbidden images that came as she held Jake close. She had almost forgotten why they were standing in the darkened tasting room, Jake with a loaded gun in her hand, until Jake reached up and yanked Cara's hand away from her mouth.

"Damn it, Cara, what do you think you doing?" she seethed in a whisper.

Another noise jolted both women back to the reality of the situation and the possible danger. Jake pulled away from Cara and angrily gestured for her to stay put, but Cara shook her head no. Exasperated, but with no time to argue, Jake pinned Cara to the wall behind her and in a hushed voice hissed, "You will stay here."

Jake frantically tried to process the situation. She knew nothing could get past the hidden cameras she had planted, and so far she hadn't seen anything suspicious on the monitor or the tapes. If someone was placing cocaine in the false bottoms of the barrels, she didn't want to blow the surveillance by making her presence known. Not when the task force was getting this close to flushing out and shutting down not only the Mexican connection, but a major drug trafficking organization in Colombia.

Thoughts were racing through Jake's gray matter faster than the speed of light. She didn't know how Cara would react if the culprit turned out to be one of her brothers. Would she be able to contain herself and follow Jake's lead? Jake couldn't be sure, knowing how headstrong Cara was. *Damn woman hasn't changed a bit, not a goddamn bit. She is still as arrogant as she ever was. Unreasonable, stubborn, impossible—well, let's hope it's just an unsuspecting burglar who unfortunately chose the wrong place and the wrong time to break in. We probably chased him the hell away anyway with all the noise we were making.*

Another noise behind them startled both women. Jake swung around to see Tiana standing in her stocking feet looking up at them. If her stare hadn't been focused on the gun in Jake's hand, it would have been comical; most of what Jake could see of her was covered in chocolate.

"Aunt Cara, is something wrong?" The little girl's lip quivered, and she looked as if she was about to cry. Cara stepped in front of Jake to hide the pistol and swept the little girl up into her arms. Tiana threw her arms around her aunt's neck and burst into tears.

"Baby, what are you doing here? Your mother must be looking all over for you. Honey, why are you crying?"

"Aunt Cara, please don't be mad at me. Hattie told me not to be sliding across the waxed floors, but..." Tiana's grip on Cara's neck tightened as her tear-filled eyes glanced at a toppled wine display and an array of wine bottles scattered across the floor.

Tears streaked through chocolate-covered cheeks as Tiana sobbed. "Is Jake mad at you, Aunt Cara?"

Cara looked to Jake, at a loss for words. "Uh, no, honey, we were just—uh..."

Jake tucked the gun under her jacket in the back of her waistband. "We were practicing, uh, self-defense. I was showing your aunt a hold I learned. Right, Cara?"

Cara's eyebrow went up and her brown eyes relayed her gratitude. "Yep, that's right, honey, Jake was showing me how to protect myself."

Tiana relaxed in her aunt's arms, and her face brightened. "Really," she hiccupped, "Aunt Cara? Will you show me too," another hiccup, "Jake?"

An ache filled Jake's heart as she smiled at the little girl in Cara's arms; she looked so much like her aunt. Jake couldn't help but think that they might have had a child like Tiana. She pushed a lock of Tiana's hair from her eyes just as she used to do with Cara's. Sad hazel eyes locked on Cara's knowing brown ones, and Jake's voice was husky with emotion.

"Sure, Tiana, I sure will, honey."

Cara could see the hazel eyes she loved fill with moisture. "Hey, how about we get this cleaned up before your mom comes looking for you? Go put your shoes on, and I'll get a broom to sweep up the glass, okay?"

Tiana wriggled out of Cara's arms and ran to get her shoes, leaving her aunt alone with Jake. The two women stood looking at each other as eyes searched and questioned.

Jake spoke first. "What were you doing here this time of evening? You usually work in your office in the house after dinner."

Cara wanted to close the space between them, take Jake into her arms, and tell her everything. Just when she thought that she might, Tiana came running back into the room, and Jake bent over to pick up the display case.

"I was in my office going over the preparation checklist for the open house tomorrow, making sure I've taken care of all the last-minute details."

The voice in Jake's head repeated itself as if trying to convince her. *I will not let her get to me. I am not going to let her get to me.* "Uh, good. I'll just get the broom so we can get this cleaned up."

Kate showed McKenzie to the guesthouse, and on her way back to look for Jake to inform her that her guest had arrived, ran into Maggie, who was on her way to the tasting room to look for Tiana. Seeing that Jake's car was in its parking place, Maggie told Kate she would deliver the message. Stephen was down for the night and, as usual, it was well past Tiana's bedtime. Cara was

117

working late in her office at the tasting room, so most likely that was where Tiana would be found.

A troubled look etched Maggie's normally flawless features and an unwelcome feeling settled in her stomach as she watched the scene from the window. Tiana was sitting on the bar watching her aunt and Jake clean up a downed display case and a heap of scattered bottles.

Oh, Tiana, what have you been up to? The little girl was always getting into mischief, but that wasn't what bothered Maggie. It was the looks passing between the two women when each thought the other wasn't watching. She had sensed it before, beneath Jake's cool demeanor and simmering anger, and she'd seen that faraway look in Cara's eyes and on her face every time Jake was near or Jake's name was mentioned.

The tension between the two was obvious. To most, it could be construed as a mutual dislike. Maggie wasn't so sure it was that simple. She hadn't wanted to face it, but the physical attraction between the two was definitely there—like a charge of electricity, circling, as opposite charges shot out toward each other, desperate to connect.

"Ouch. Damn." Jake grabbed her index finger as blood spurted out around a piece of glass.

Cara darted, first to the bar to fetch a towel, then back over to Jake. "Here, let me see it, Jake."

"It's all right, just a piece of glass."

Cara gently took the bleeding finger, ignoring Jake's attempt to take the towel from her. "Hush, quit fussing. Stand still and let me pull the glass out so we can flush it out."

"It's not that bad. I can just get it out when we're through here."

Jake felt warmth creeping through her entire body as Cara shifted closer to view her finger. "I see it, just let me..." She quickly pulled the piece of glass out and was still holding Jake's hand, applying pressure to the wound, when Maggie entered the room.

"Did someone get hurt?" Cara's closeness to Jake was making Maggie uncomfortable, and Jake could see it in her attitude and posture. She moved away from Cara and wrapped the towel around her hand.

Cara winked at Tiana, then smiled at Maggie. "Nothing serious. Jake had a piece of glass in her finger, but it's out now."

Maggie moved to stand close beside Cara and whispered, "You spoil her, you know." Then she directed her attention to Jake. "Jacquelyn, you have a visitor. A McKenzie Quinn. I believe we...ran into to you both in San Diego. Kate showed her to the guesthouse. I hope that was all right? She said you were expecting her."

Jake nervously looked at her watch, then at Maggie, avoiding Cara's blatant, questioning stare. "You did, thank you, yes, and I am," Jake rattled off. "If, uh, you can finish up here, Cara, I will see you all in the morning."

"Jacquelyn, the guesthouse is small and only has the one bedroom. If your guest would like to stay at the house, we have more than enough room. She's most welcome."

Jake just wanted to get out of the room; she could feel Cara's eyes boring a hole right through her. "Uh, no, uh, she—thank you, I'll ask her." Jake's face softened as she looked at Tiana sitting on the bar watching the three adults curiously. "Good night, Tiana. We'll work on that move, okay?"

Tiana shook her head, eagerly trying to fight off the sleepiness of her busy day.

Cara felt her gut churning with jealousy as Jake hurried out and down the path toward another woman. She walked over and scooped up a very tired little girl. "The workmen can reset this display in the morning. Come on, Tiana, let's get you to bed."

Half asleep, the little girl snuggled into her aunt's warm arms. "Aunt Cara, do you think Jake will really teach me how to protect myself too?" she asked drowsily, her head snuggled warmly into Cara's neck.

Before Cara could answer, Tiana was fast asleep.

Cara looked down at her niece with a fond smile. "She'll be lucky if she doesn't keep us awake with a bellyache from all the chocolate she was into. And while she will recover from all her excitement, I'm afraid her favorite yellow shirt has met its end."

Maggie laughed, pointing to the stains on Cara's silk blouse. "Well, we might say the same about yours."

Chuckling, Cara looked down at her blouse, then tucked Tiana's arms tighter around her neck and reached for Maggie's hand. "We've all had a long day. Come on, let's go get her to bed."

There was little conversation as Cara carried the sleeping Tiana along the trail through the vineyards to the main house. After she and Maggie had settled Tiana in her bed with a good-night kiss, Cara went to the adjoining room to check on the baby. Stephen was sleeping soundly and probably wouldn't wake for a few hours for his next feeding.

Cara leaned over the crib and gently smoothed the soft, dark tufts of hair on his head, then fussed a little, straightening his blanket. Her heart filled with love each time she looked at the tiny fingers that reached out even in sleep to curl around her little finger. The baby sighed and blew tiny bubbles that stayed on his dainty pink lips as Cara stroked his cheek.

"I love you, my son, with all my heart, and I will always keep you safe, I promise."

She kissed her sleeping child, then turned on the small lamp and walked out onto the veranda. She had so much on her mind, and most of it involved Jake.

CHAPTER NINETEEN

Since Cara had returned home to Cipriano, Maggie had sensed that more was bothering her than the turmoil of coming home. Tonight was different; tonight Cara was on edge and restless, and she paced like a caged tigress. Lately, she hadn't wanted to talk, and Maggie missed that special time alone after the children were down for the night. Cara always liked to sit and listen while Maggie told her everything about Stephen's day.

Maggie had never asked who Stephen's father was. She knew Cara would tell her when she was ready. One thing she did know for sure: it wasn't a longing for Stephen's father that put the sadness in her friend's eyes—the same sadness that the brown eyes could not hide when she looked at Jacquelyn.

She wondered where Cara and Jacquelyn had first met and what the history was behind McKenzie Quinn's remarks in San Diego. The incident had happened so fast it was hard to tell, but Maggie would have sworn she saw the weighty tell of hurt behind those otherwise impassive hazel eyes. She questioned whether Cara's mood was connected with the arrival of her new assistant. *If they hadn't been at odds with each other from day one in San Diego and every day since her arrival here, I would think Cara was jealous that she has a guest staying with her tonight!*

She opened the twin doors of her bedroom leading out to the veranda to let in the evening breeze off the ocean and went to draw a hot bath before retiring.

Her head rested on the edge of the clawfoot tub as Maggie relished in a long, leisurely soak. All the thoughts about her relationship with her best friend were pounding at her temples. She had loved Cara since forever; it had always been. Cara had taken her by the hand to first grade, punched the first boy who was mean, and taught her how to ride her first pony. They had giggled while Maggie tried on her first training bra and shared their innermost secrets of pubescent yearnings.

Both Maggie and Cara grew to be stunning women, neither lacking attention from the opposite sex. Cara was never interested in boys or dating, and Maggie was content just to be one of the three musketeers. It was always just the three of them—Cara, Stephen, and Maggie—until that night on the beach and the end of summer vacation right before Cara went off to college.

Maggie knew that Cara's lovers throughout her college years had been women. Paolo had made sure that everyone knew, especially Cara's grandfather. Maggie had known for a long time that her feelings for Cara ran much deeper than those of a best friend. She wanted to share every day and night for the rest of her life with Cara, including her bed.

A crescent moon cast spectral slivers of white across the still of the night. Cara's shoulder-length dark hair blew gently around her face as she stared in the direction of the guesthouse, agitated by McKenzie's arrival. She knew she was being unreasonable in her fears, but her heart had never read the message that Jake was no longer hers. She continued to pace as the burning image of Jake lying in the arms of another woman tormented her.

McKenzie! How in the hell did McKenzie get into the picture? She thought about how protective McKenzie had been toward Jake in San Diego. She closed her eyes, trying to shut out the picture of McKenzie putting her arm so possessively around Jake's waist. *That was more than just friendship!* Cara didn't know how to deal with her jealously, and the longing for Jake was unbearable. She trembled as a whisper of a breeze blew across her skin, and with the breeze came the memory of another time, another place, and of Jake's gentle passion.

She straddled the intruder lying beneath her on the threadbare carpet of the hotel room, pressing the barrel of the gun hard against the intruder's head. The sporadic flicker of the neon sign outside the window, like a silent motion picture, illuminated the face a millisecond just before Cara tightened her finger on the trigger. It was Jake lying on the floor.

Cara began to hyperventilate, and her heart pounded wildly against her chest. "Oh God! I could have..."

Jake slid her arms around Cara's waist, holding her tightly to convince her she was all right, then silenced her fear with a gentle yet passionate kiss and whispered softly into her ear. "Have I ever told you talk too much, Counselor?"

She vaguely remembered lifting Jake off the floor and carrying her to the bed. They touched and explored each other with a hunger rising from deep within their souls, joining desire and love. Each giving and taking until the dawn of day found them entwined and exhausted, the very essence of each indelibly etched forever upon the sated soul of the other.

The memory of Jake's kiss left in its wake an agonizing tension. Every nerve ending was taut and hypersensitive, her stomach tensed in knots. Cara wanted Jake, ached for the touch of her skin against hers and the sound of her voice caressing her deep in the night. She didn't want McKenzie touching Jake or seeing her hazel eyes turn hazy green with desire. That was only for her.

There had not been a moment since Cara had left the ranch in Arizona that she hadn't wanted Jake by her side. Her pregnancy had not been an easy one. Constant morning sickness had led to dehydration and hospitalization for IV fluid replacement. Breakthrough bleeding at thirty-two weeks and the threat of a premature delivery kept her on strict bed rest until she delivered Stephen at thirty-six weeks. Although he was premature, the use of betamethasone while he was still in the womb had helped his lungs to develop enough so that he had not been put on a ventilator.

Cara had needed Jake during the long days and nights that she sat beside his incubator in the NICU, singing softly, touching and calming him, letting him know he was wanted and loved. The day she was able to breast-feed Stephen for the first time brought tears of joy for the little man she held in her arms—and for the loss of all that could have been.

It seemed to be a night for restlessness as Maggie wandered out onto the veranda, hoping the glass of wine she'd poured would help her relax enough to sleep. The distance she felt between herself and Cara earlier bothered her, and she contemplated going to talk to her about it. She could see a low light coming from Cara's bedroom. Then, as her eyes adjusted to the dark, she could see Cara standing with a forlorn, deserted look on her face, her arms wrapped tightly around herself as she stared out into the night.

More than I need to be with her, she needs her space tonight to deal with whatever it is that is eating away at her. Our talk can wait until tomorrow; maybe we will all be in a better mood.

The well-dressed olive-skinned man stood scrutinizing the colored pins sticking out of the detailed map on the wall of the opulent room, his black eyes narrowing menacingly. Two men behind him exchanged worried glances and shifted their weight uncomfortably as beads of sweat formed across their brows and upper lips.

"All the shipments have been moving through well, without problem. Except for this area," he said, tapping the map, "here."

Both men had seen the aftermath of his anger when he was displeased, and neither wanted to be on the receiving end. Hector stepped forward, twisting his hat nervously in his shaking hands.

"There has been a slight problem with that location, *Jefe*."

A finger traced along the map of the coast of Southern California. "And why is that, Hector? Can you explain this to me?"

Hector struggled to form his words, fear sucking the moisture from his mouth, numbing his tongue and mind. He knew that his life meant nothing to the man with the piercing devil eyes—failure could cost him his life. If it was his time, he prayed to the Lady of Guadalupe for it to be merciful and quick.

"Guido, can you help Hector here explain to me why the shipment to here..." A flash from the thin bladed knife that left Sandro's hand and stuck out of the map was all either man saw. "...has not been delivered."

Guido forced the words from his gut. "*Señor* Sandro, it has been difficult since the *cabeza de la familia* has returned. The woman, she has eyes in the back of her head and never sleeps."

"I see. So, let me get this straight. You let a woman—one woman—interfere?"

"No, *Jefe*, no. Our contact assures us it is temporary and that there will be no further problems."

"Good, but for now, I do not want any unnecessary attention drawn to this area. Is that understood? What do you know about this woman? This woman, who has made you all look like the impotent sheep you are."

Sandro pulled the knife from the map; walking over to stand in front of Hector, he pressed the knife tip against the hollow of his throat. Frozen with fear, not that he was about to die, but that his death would be tortuous, the quivering man looked into an inferno. Eyes that revealed the fires of hell pierced him as sharply as the knife. Blood-red drops fell in slow motion and splattered down the front of his white shirt. Sandro's venomous smile and the aura surrounding him personified evil. His handsome human form was merely the embodiment *el diablo* on earth, in the flesh.

"You will find out everything you can about this woman, this *mujer jefe*. Is that not so, Hector? I want to know how many pesos are in her bank account. I want to know when she yawns, when she sneezes, and who she fucks. *Usted entiende?*"

Hector could not answer. The tip of the blade was pressing into his windpipe, and with any movement, its razor sharpness would sever the thin-walled, cartilaginous tube.

Evil had long ago consumed Sandro's soul, feeding off the fear and the perversity of humankind. He toyed with the man but controlled his anger. He would deal with the incompetence at another time, for he was feeling generous—and he had a job for them to do.

Sandro removed the knife from Hector's throat and went back to studying the map. "Get out of my sight, and do not return until you have the information I want."

He poured himself another tequila, watching the liquor trickle into the glass. As he cleared his mind, his eyes focused on the map and the coast of California. The delay of the last few deliveries of cocaine did not concern him as much as the nameless, faceless woman did. His gut tightened. It was the area that had been chosen, and there could not be a problem; too much was at stake. A grinning sneer hardened his face as his voice echoed across the room.

"Who are you, boss lady? And what is your weakness? What is it that you most value?" The evil grin reflected his inner thoughts as a feeling of anticipation of the game stirred in his loins. "Can you be bought?"

He finished his drink and poured another, holding the golden liquid up to the light. "What is your price? Soon enough, I will know."

CHAPTER TWENTY

Harry Sweeney's words slammed into Matt's gut, sending waves of adrenaline into his blood. This was the first viable lead in over a year that placed Sandro north of the border. Months of unrelenting investigation following any lead and analyzing as much as a nickel bag of coke had confirmed Sandro's connection to the Rivera drug trafficking in the United States. Now he was across the border and in Southern California.

The very core of Matt's innate sense of right and wrong clamored for justice in accordance with the law, but the taste for revenge was bitter in his mouth. Sandro's malignancy had touched the lives of those he cared about—his mother, Jake, Jake's father, Jack Biscayne, and Alejandro, Matt's partner and Craig's brother. The explosion that killed Jake's fiancé, Sam, had been linked to an investigation of the Colombian connection and the Rivera drug cartel. The evil dressed in lamb's clothing had walked the deserts of Kuwait, Mexico, and Arizona, raping and mutilating as he went, leaving a grisly swath of death in his wake.

Matt could not share any information about the task force and Operation Monsoon Rain with Harry without first consulting with SAC Josh McNeil. But if the evidence confirmed that Sandro was the killer, Harry would be a valuable resource and addition to the team. A sudden jolt of fear burned Matt's thoughts like a hot branding iron as his callused hand tightened around the phone.

Sandro's in California. Jake! If Sandro connects her— Jesus—and Cara, they're both dead! Matt threw his duffel in the back of the truck and sped down the dirt road, leaving a trail of dust behind.

The sun was casting monochrome colors of early dawn when he pulled up in front of Maria's Café. He knew his mother would be there, as she always was before sunup, preparing the dough and simmering the soup for the day's menu.

He sat with both hands gripping the steering wheel looking down the street toward the office Kalani shared with Jake. This past year had been hard—equally hard on all of them, for different reasons. Learning that Teresa was his daughter after one night with Kalani years ago, and his developing relationship with them, had been his anchor. He suspected Kalani was in love with him and wanted more, to be a family. They were close to taking it to the next level of intimacy, but each time they reached that point, he backed off. He wanted her, but he had to be sure that his feelings for Jake were put away. Kalani was too good a woman and deserved nothing less.

Any man would want Kalani; she is beautiful, thoughtful, and a damn good mother. Still, his heart had pounded against his chest at the prospect of Jake being in danger when Harry had told him about the murders in L.A. *Ah hell, Jake! How do I stop loving you?* Matt open the door of the truck, hesitated as if at a crossroads, then walked toward the café.

Maria glanced up from the dough she was kneading and looked across the open serving window between the kitchen and the counter. Matt's voice was gruff but filled with affection for his mother. "*Madre*, how many times do I need to tell you to lock the door when you are alone! Anyone could just waltz in here."

Maria's eyes had grown tired and her step a mite slower this past year. Matt knew that learning Teresa was her grandchild was the saving factor that had kept his mother going. There had always been a special bond and affection between his mother and Teresa, and it had grown even stronger.

Maria looked at the handsome, rugged face of her son. His hair was beginning to gray at the temples and his smile was less quick these days, but his pale blue eyes still reflected a caring heart.

"Who, pray tell, made you my keeper, Matt Peyson? I have been coming in to prepare the dough at the same time every day for twenty-five years, and nobody has carried me off yet." For emphasis, she slapped the dough onto the board, expressing her indignation in her native tongue.

Matt shook his head, distracted, and Maria, realizing that he was not in uniform, sensed that he had something on his mind. She added more flour and started to roll out the dough while Matt poured himself a cup of coffee.

"You might as well tell me and get it off your chest, *mi hijo*."

Matt chuckled and smiled; he never could hide anything from Maria. "*Madre*, you missed your calling. You should have hung a shingle and dealt the cards."

He could have kicked himself as soon as the words were out of his mouth. It was Sandro's favorite phrase when Maria uncannily always seemed to know when they were up to mischief or into something they shouldn't have been. Maria did read the tarot cards, as her mother had before her, and as her grandmother had before that. As far as Matt knew, she hadn't read the cards in a long time.

He studied the sadness in her faded brown eyes and the new lines that grief had put on her face as she put the pan of cinnamon rolls in to bake. "I stopped to tell you I will be gone for a few days—a while maybe."

Matt sipped his coffee, deep in thought, looking out at the awakening streets of Nogales. He wondered if this was where he wanted Teresa to grow up. Only a week earlier, the border patrol closed down another tunnel from Sonora, Mexico, into Nogales that was used to smuggle contraband such as illegal immigrants, firearms, and vast amounts of prescription and illegal drugs. It was never-ending—and insurmountable. Even before they closed one, another was being dug to replace it.

"*Madre*, keep an eye on Teresa and Kalani for me until I get back."

Maria's heart warmed at the love in her son's voice when he spoke of his daughter. Still, there was something in Matt's eyes and the determined look along his jaw that frightened her. "Does this trip have anything to do with Sandro?"

The name, unspoken by either of them to the other in over a year, hung suspended in the stillness like a spider dangling from its web. A chilled waft of air moved across the café between them as they faced the demon.

Matt thought, just for a moment, about not telling his mother the truth, but he had never lied to her before and he wouldn't start now. He took a deep breath, not turning away from the deceptive placidity of the awakening small border town.

"Harry Sweeney called me last night from L.A. He is investigating a triple murder that might be linked to illegal drug trafficking in Southern California. The way..." Matt's voice faltered slightly. "The way they were tortured and killed—well, he's pretty sure it could be Sandro."

Matt set his coffee cup down, picked up his brown Stetson, and walked over to his mother. Putting his arms around her, he saw the worried look on her face as he leaned down to kiss her cheek. "I'll be back when this is over, Mama. I promise. I left a note for Teresa and Kalani. It's too early to wake them up. Tell them that I—just tell them I'll be back."

Maria's worried eyes watched her son as he walked out the door, and her hand reached into her apron pocket to pull out the deck of tarot cards. She shuffled the cards, turned over the first of three, and laid it on the counter. Justice, sword lifted high in the right and the balancing scale in the left.

An icy finger ran down her spine, making her shiver in anticipation of the next card. Her eyes froze on the images. The second card revealed the Devil, a horned apparition, goat faced with eagle's claws as feet, and mankind bound by chains beneath him. The last and third card was Death, reversed, an armored skeleton sitting atop a white horse ambling his way past a fallen king.

Maria considered the omen of the cards. Did they foretell the endless, fated battle between good and evil, darkness and the light? What side of the scale of justice would the fates and destiny favor?

Maria fingers paused on the next unturned card, and her gaze remained frozen on the intricate pattern on the back. As if by a will of their own, her hands gathered the cards and set them aside. She touched the cup Matt had been drinking from, and her tired brown eyes filled with tears.

"Be careful and come home when you are finished, *mi hijo*."

CHAPTER TWENTY-ONE

The annual Vintners' Harvest Festival was well underway, and Santa Barbara and Cipriano Vineyards took on a holiday atmosphere. Everyone was busy greeting visitors, conducting tours, or working in the tasting room. Paulo and Giancarlo were out in the vineyard with groups that had reserved tours of the prestigious Cipriano Vineyards as much as a year in advance. Maggie was working the tasting room, and Jake was escorting a group through the fermentation and aging room. Cara was everywhere, facilitating things and making sure it all was running smoothly.

The cool ocean breeze, unique to Santa Barbara's coastal range and helping to shape the rich viticulture microclimate, caressed the valley and the vineyards. It was a perfect day.

Sulking, Tiana sat with her grandfather on the veranda as he watched the activities below. "Grandfather, why can't I just go and help Aunt Cara? I promise I won't get in the way," she pouted.

Sebastian smiled and lifted his face to the warm sun remembering how Cara, when she was Tiana's age, would sneak away from Hattie during festival time and follow by his side all day, anxious to experience and learn everything.

"*Mia bell'impaziente,* Tiana, you will stay here. Sorrin needs your help with Stephen. Now, go ask Hattie to fix us tea and a tray of her delicious cannolis and later, maybe, Cara will need your help preparing for the dinner and dance tonight."

Tiana jumped up excitedly from her chair, her brown eyes filled with hope. "Grandfather, will I be allowed to go to the dance, please, just for a little while?"

Sebastian's eyes twinkled with amusement as his great-granddaughter ran toward the stairway. "Tiana, ask Hattie to put a little brandy in mine."

Tiana stomped her foot. "You know, Grandfather, she will not let me bring you brandy. I'm just a little kid."

Sebastian roared with laughter. "Go, get the tea. Do you have a dress to wear, Tiana, *la mia ragazza piccola*?"

Tiana stopped dead in her tracks and turned around with a puzzled scowl on her face as she surveyed her blue jeans and sneakers. "A dress, Grandfather?"

"*Sì*, a dress. The young ladies I escort to a dance usually do wear a dress, Tiana. You do have one?"

The sharp mind of the five-year-old solved the dilemma quickly. "Grandfather, not to worry, I will escort you." Then she ran eagerly down the stairs and toward the kitchen.

Jake was having a hard time concentrating as she prepared to escort her group through the winery. She could smell the aroma of coffee coming from the large urns set up for the guests and hoped a cup would help get her body and her mind in gear. It had been a long night, one that left her with little sleep, too many questions, and not enough answers.

The possibility of a major drug drop, complicated by not knowing the identity of the inside connection at Cipriano and the danger it put everyone in, had Jake constantly scanning the faces of the guests and the many workers hired just for the event. Looking for—what? Nothing had indicated a drop had been made, and the hidden surveillance cameras had not picked up any suspicious activity. The undercover agents scattered throughout the vineyards posing as workers had not reported any activities or movements that appeared out of the ordinary. If there were any, she questioned if it would be wise to go ahead with the activities. And if Cipriano withdrew from the festival without justification, would it be too suspicious and jeopardize the entire operation? Josh McNeil had left it up to her; it was her call.

The Mexican cartel had been forced to devise ingenious ways to smuggle their poison into the U.S. since the heightened terrorist security at the borders following the events of 9/11. The festivities and the thousands of people who came by land and by sea to enjoy the events at the various vineyards and Santa Barbara were a perfect screen for a drop. Yachts of all sizes in the various harbors and anchored in the coastal waters along the shoreline were too numerous to count. The event attracted devoted wine connoisseurs along with average tourists and the very wealthy. It was a major party time, and the cartel could simply use the crowds to blend in.

The task force knew the history. The smugglers wouldn't just drop millions in drugs and leave them unattended until the money exchanged hands and the drugs went to their next destination. Anything could happen, even an all-out bloodbath if the cartel or their counterpart here in the States suspected anything. Many innocent civilians could be hurt or killed.

Jake sighed and looked at her watch; it was time to start her tour, and she hadn't seen McKenzie yet that morning. It seemed she was making it a habit of leaving before McKenzie woke. She had promised McKenzie the previous night that they would have lunch together and talk. She berated herself for bringing McKenzie into the situation, but when she'd seen Cara with Maggie she impulsively had called her.

McNeil's earlier question taunted her: was her relationship with Cara influencing her judgment and compromising the entire operation? *You need to deal with it, Jake. You've tried to distance your feelings for Cara. She's arrogant and impossible and she continues to devastate your heart, but you're still in love with her, and seeing her with Maggie every day is driving you plain crazy. Get through this weekend, then talk to McNeil and have him replace you.*

Cara never missed her early morning ride along the rows of grapevines, and this day was no exception. She rode the fields as her grandfather had as the sun came up each day over Cipriano.

Even as a little girl when she would get up before dawn to ride with her grandfather, she had loved the smell of the earth, the sun and mist from the ocean mingling, unfurling the bouquet of promise within the grape. As a child she had thought it mystical how the clouds of fog would caress and play with the vines, then disappear back to the ocean as the sun chased them away.

Still dressed in riding pants and boots, she went to the main house to check on Grandfather and Stephen, pleased that Sorrin hadn't fed Stephen the milk she'd expressed that morning. When she could, she preferred feeding him from her breast. It was the time of day she cherished the most, sitting in the rocker holding and nursing Stephen. She watched in awe and wonder at such perfection and thrilled with his ever-changing expressions. After settling Stephen down for a nap, she went to find Tiana to tell one very excited little girl she could join the dancing for a while after dinner.

She was about to leave to go to the tasting room after stopping in the main house to pick up some papers on her office desk when the door opened. She looked up to familiar green eyes that portrayed the ire of the redhead standing in the doorway.

"We need to talk."

Seeing McKenzie standing there, as attractive as ever, just piqued the feeling of jealousy Cara had felt all night. She struggled to control the pent-up frustration that was seething just beneath the surface, threatening to unleash on the petite redhead. She couldn't hide the abruptness in her voice, and she knew that a confrontation with McKenzie would lead to angry words. "Now is not a good time, McKenzie. You shouldn't even be here."

"Oh really, now, Cara Vittore—excuse me, Cipriano. And just when would you be sayin' a good time might be? As far as being here, Jacquelyn invited me. I know there is something going on; what I don't know is where you and Cipriano come into it. But if she needs me, this is where I'll be, without question."

Cara slammed the papers down on her desk, then immediately checked her temper. *What in the hell is wrong with Jake, bringing McKenzie here?* "We have nothing to talk about, Kenzie, so let's just leave it."

Five foot three inches of Irish determination focused on Cara. "I don't know the story behind you and Jacquelyn or why you left her. It's not important. But you hurt her, Cara. She opened her heart to you, gave you her trust and her love, and you betrayed that trust and a most precious love. It's only fair that I tell you: if she'll let me, I want to be in her life. I want to love her and be with her and work on putting our lives together. If she will give me the chance, I know I can make her happy."

Cara's eyes showed no protest as they filled with tears. Her tense body posture eased. "She deserves all the happiness and love you can give her, McKenzie, and so much more."

McKenzie's green eyes softened and her anger ebbed as she watched the emotion in Cara's eyes. Something about her was different. She was still the beautiful woman McKenzie had loved and mentored through law school—even more beautiful, if that were possible. She looked tired, but there was something more. Her brown eyes reflected a naked sorrow, a vulnerability that McKenzie had never seen in her before.

McKenzie realized she couldn't fight with this woman and she didn't hate her; after all, they had been lovers as well as friends. "We've shared much, my friend, and my heart tells me you had your reasons for leaving the way you did."

Two old friends locked eyes as an unspoken truce passed between them. Emotion tugged at McKenzie's heart; a part of her would always love the woman who stood before her.

"I never thought I could love anyone as much as I did you. I should have come after you when you left Boston, but we were both too young and too concerned with our careers to see what we could have had. When I finally had the time and realized you were the only one in my heart, it was too late. We both had gone on with our careers and lives. When you left my bed that night in Tucson, I knew you were in love with Jake. Ironic, isn't it? Both of us loving the same woman."

The sadness in McKenzie's deep green eyes mimicked the sadness of her small smile as she quietly turned and left.

Cara stared into the palpable emptiness of the space around her. Her soul could not find sanctuary or refuge from the sense of loss in her life that at that moment was unbearable. Stephen's loss, Grandfather's illness and the years of estrangement, her brothers' enmity—and McKenzie with the woman she loved more than her own life—all were crashing down around her. McKenzie would give Jake everything she had been unable to give. She would be there for her, to cherishing and protecting her heart.

Every fiber of Cara's being was reaching out for Jake. She needed her just as she needed the ragged burning breath she now struggled to take into her lungs. Would it make a difference if she went to Jake and told her everything? Could there be a chance she would understand? Could she forgive? Cara had never let go of the impossible longing that had helped her survive the aftermath of Mexico: the hope that she and Jake would be together again one day after all of this was over. It was her dream, but she knew it was time to face reality. Jake had gone on with her life.

Cara felt an overwhelming sense of guilt for the choices and paths she had taken. Was it the supposed force of fate or a self-fulfilling destiny? Grandfather, the children, Maggie—they all needed her. Cipriano needed her.

She ran her hand through her thick, dark hair. Her brothers resented her. If it was one or both of them running the drugs out of Cipriano, was it her fault? Grandfather had chosen her over both of them—could she live with herself if the task force closed the net and one or both of her brothers were imprisoned or killed or someone else got hurt? It would undoubtedly kill her grandfather.

The undercover operation no longer mattered. She would confront Paulo and Giancarlo and give them both a choice, a chance. It was insane to put Grandfather, Maggie, and the children in harm's way for any reason. A look of defiance and renewed strength replaced the beaten look in Cara's eyes as her fist came down hard on the top of the desk.

"Damn destiny!"

It was time to challenge the fates and take control. She squared her shoulders and picked up the phone, dialing Rachel Slade at the attorney general's office.

"I need to speak to her today. It is of the utmost importance. Is there a number where I can reach her? Please, have her return my call as soon as possible. Yes, she does have the number."

I need to talk to Jake. She needs to know of my decision.

CHAPTER TWENTY-TWO

"Any questions?"
"Yes, I have one, please."

Jake's eyes focused on a slightly built Oriental man standing toward the back of the group. A small flicker of recognition crossed her mind but left just as fast.

"What does the term *corked wine* mean, and are more winemakers going to the synthetic cork?"

Jake smiled. "Ah, a term often misunderstood by wine enthusiasts. Simply put, the term means that a bad cork has ruined a good bottle of wine by an invisible mold that has grown within the pores of the cork. That, combined with traces of the bleach used to treat the cork, taint the wine."

Laughing, Jake made a face. "It is a dreadful smell. Kind of, well, in my opinion, reminiscent of wet socks. When a wine tastes flat, it can be the same mold, just less severe. Please don't confuse a cork-wine mold, which is invisible, with the mold you might see under the capsule on top of the cork. That's caused by a bit of leakage, no harm, just wipe it off before you pour.

"Synthetic cork? Yes, many are, especially here in the States, and more vineyards will do so as wine lovers accept the fact that a synthetic cork does not mean a lesser quality wine. Great questions. Now if you will follow me, we can view the fermentation room."

Jake led the group through the open doors of the reception area adjacent to the tasting room, across an open terrace designed to allow fledgling wine tasters and wine connoisseurs alike a view of the romantic and tranquil scenery of Cipriano. It was a picture out of old Italy, with its hanging bougainvillea and picturesque oak-lined roads, gentle rolling hills, and grapevines. Workers, bent with their heads and eyes protected by straw hats, tended to the vines while the sounds of seagulls floated on the freshening breeze.

The day was warm, cloudless, with endless blue skies. As Jake led the tour along the cobblestone pathway into the fermentation room, explaining the advantages of stainless steel tanks, she suddenly felt an icy chill and goose bumps rising along her arms. It was the same feeling she'd had the day her father and fiancé were killed, as if something or someone evil had walked across their graves. Her heart lurched in her chest as a sense of foreboding washed over her. The feeling that someone she cared about was in danger was so strong that she shivered as her senses heightened.

She immediately scanned the faces of the group she was leading. Was the danger in the room? Now? Someone was talking, but it sounded far away, dreamy. Something was wrong and she couldn't explain it, but her every instinct was on full alert. She couldn't shake the feeling something was about to happen, and the uneasiness distracted her attention from the people in her group, who were looking at her rather strangely. As her panic began to tighten its grip, her eyes were drawn inexplicably to a concerned brown gaze that reached across the room, apparently also sensing that something was terribly wrong.

Cara had caught up with Jake just as they were entering the next stop on the tour. Marnie, an assistant who worked in the tasting room, would conduct the next and last part of the tour, so it was a good time to ask Jake to come to her office. Cara knew that her decision could put the operation and the Monsoon Rain task force at risk of being exposed, or at the very least, set back the investigation. She also knew that Jake's reaction would not be positive, but she was adamant about her decision and would personally assure Rachel Slade and Josh McNeil that no one, including her brothers, would know of the existence of the covert operation. If McNeil's sources were right, if something big was going down and the drugs were dropped at Cipriano this weekend, all anyone needed to know was that the drugs were discovered randomly and they were turned over to the authorities.

Cara watched the graceful way Jake moved her hands as she talked, using her delicate long fingers to emphasis a point. She had always loved how Jake tilted her head with just the hint of a smile when listening or absorbed in what she was doing. At times like these, when Jake was relaxed and unaware she was being observed, Cara felt the pain, the loss of sharing a life with the beautiful doctor, more acutely. Cara watched as Jake suddenly faltered, turning pale, then stopped talking in the middle of answering a question.

Cara waited a few moments, keenly aware of Jake's distress, then drew the group's attention to the other side of the room and to herself. Jake's eyes locked onto Cara's and as soon as Cara's soothing voice reached past her premonition, she could feel her pounding heart begin to calm. "To answer your last question, larger wineries will use stainless steel tanks for fermentation because the tanks are temperature controlled by cooling coils that allow the winemaker to control the heat produced during the process." Cara kept her eyes riveted to Jake's, but continued her explanation.

"Fermentation is the process in which yeast consumes the sugar in the grape juice, converting it into carbon dioxide and alcohol. This process can be very hot. By hot, I mean temperatures in the 90s. If the temperature gets out of control, it can harm the wine. Another advantage to stainless steel tanks is that they are easily sterilized."

As Cara spoke, she moved slowly toward Jake, who was as white as a ghost. She fought to keep from running to her while trying to concentrate and talk. "So, for the most part, the higher the Brix, meaning sugar content, at harvest—and it's usually somewhere around 24-27 Brix, depending on what the grower and winemaker decide—the higher the alcohol. When fermentation is complete, the wine is dry, or as the Italians say, *vino secco*."

Pointing to a woman standing in front, she said, "To answer your question, *sweet wine* simply means fermentation was halted and there is a bit of residual sugar left in the wine." Cara knew she was rushing the group through the tour, but something was terribly wrong, and she needed to get to Jake.

"Now, if you will follow Marnie, she will show you through the aging cellars and on to the tasting room, where we have commemorative wineglasses for each of you to sample and enjoy our many special varieties of Cipriano wines. We welcome you to take your time to explore the grounds and enjoy the festivities."

Cara reached Jake just as the last person exited, neither woman noticing the Oriental man who had been lagging behind all the while.

Jake's anxiety had eased with each step Cara took toward her. Cara's concerned eyes conveyed a message of caring and—love? That one look. It was as if none of the events of the past year had happened as Cara reached her and put her arm around her shoulders to steady her and draw her into a protective embrace. She leaned into Cara for support, trusting the familiar strength, as she turned her face into Cara's neck, breathing in the fragrance of the woman who had her heart.

"Jake, what is it? Is something wrong?"

Jake hesitated. She was dizzy and unsteady. Whatever had spooked her left her shaken, weak. "I—I just...the truth is I have this feeling, the same kind of feeling I get sometimes when I'm profiling or when—" She couldn't voice the thought. "Except it's stronger and so much more intense."

Cara pulled Jake in tighter, trembling slightly. She knew Jake had uncanny instincts, and they were usually right. "Let's go into my office. Think you can make it all right?"

Jake nodded, reluctant to leave the cocoon of Cara's protecting arms. By the time they reached Cara's office, much of the effect of Jake's powerful premonition had waned, subsiding to an overall feeling of discomfort.

After handing Jake a glass of water, Cara pulled a chair over to sit across from her, but within reach. Her voice was gentle and tender. "What happened in there, Jake? Can you explain what it was that made you react that way? You said you had a feeling?"

Jake looked into Cara's brown eyes, not wanting to tell her she'd had the same feeling when Cara had been held captive and tortured by Sandro in Mexico. The memory was so close to the surface at that moment that Jake reached up to touch Cara's face with her fingertips, needing to make sure Cara was actually there and all right.

The touch of Jake's fingers on her face brought a tear to Cara's eyes, and her lonely heart wept a tear for each moment she had spent away from the other woman. Her hand trembled as it gently captured Jake's fingers against her cheek. She had whispered words of love, asking forgiveness in her dreams every night since she had left, and now a single word was hard to form. Cara searched the hazel eyes and the soul of the woman behind them, afraid that if she spoke, the moment would end.

Her voice was raspy with emotion. "Jake, there is so much I need to tell you."

Jake heard the words as she looked into eyes that told her all she needed to know. Cara hadn't left her because she didn't love her. All the anguish and hurt she had felt for the past year escaped in a sob. "Cara, why? God, when you left I...I just..."

Cara cupped Jake's face between her hands, rubbing her thumb slowly across on her cheek. "We need to talk and we need some time alone without interruption so I can explain. Please trust me until then. As much as I want to, now is not the time."

Jake's eyes, blurred with tears, searched the depth of Cara's, seeing nothing but raw honesty. "I—I want to. I tried to find you. I even used the Bureau, but all I got was stonewalled and that you were out of the country. I need to know, Cara. Why did you leave the way you did? It was something that happened in Mexico, wasn't it?"

Cara lowered her head and took in a shaky, deep breath. "Jake, when Torres and I were in that barn—"

A knock on the door stopped Cara from telling Jake everything that had happened that day in a rat-infested hole on the other side of the border and the horrific act of violence that changed their lives.

Cara looked at Jake, trying to gain the strength to get up. "I'm sorry. I will tell you everything later."

Opening the door, Cara expected to see one of the staff standing on the other side, but instead, an Oriental man carrying a battered black briefcase stood anxiously waiting.

"I am sorry to intrude, but it was the best time to get the two of you together."

Cara opened her mouth to ask who in the hell he was and what he wanted but he pushed past her into the office, putting the

141

briefcase down on the desk to open it. Cara stiffened, and Jake jumped to her feet, reaching for the gun in the holster at her waist

"Whoa, ladies, I'm just reaching for a folder here, and my ID." He laid the folder on the table and pulled his wallet out, flipping it open.

Confused, Cara looked at Jake while Jake kept her eyes on the impudent man.

"My name is Han-Kiong." He turned to Jake. "Call me Hank, and I need you to look at these pictures, Dr. Biscayne."

"Han-Kiong? I knew you looked familiar when I saw you earlier today. You're the medical examiner Philip Raynard has been working with in L.A. I met you at one of Philip's lectures last year."

"Yes, I remember. Philip has spoken in admiration of you many times, and might I add, one does not forget such a beautiful woman, Dr. Biscayne."

Jake walked to the desk with a curious look on her face and opened the folder. There it was again, the feeling that had come over her during the tour, resurgent from the pictures spread before her, images of mutilation, carnality, depravation. She had seen them before, all connecting to one name—Sandro.

Jake spoke with a strange, disjointed coldness in her voice. "Where did you get these pictures?"

"I'm sorry to spring this on you like this. I know you are undercover on assignment here, but if Matt and Harry are right, you both could be in real danger. The guy who did this might already know that the vintner C. V. Cipriano and Cara Vittore, who helped disrupt his little killing spree along the border last year, are one and the same. And from what Josh McNeil tells us, you could be sitting on a powder keg of Colombian white that belongs to him."

Cara took the pictures out of Jake's trembling hands and inhaled a pained breath at what she saw.

Han-Kiong knew from what Matt Peyson had told him that his news wasn't going to go down easy with the two women. "From what we know so far, these murders are the result of a drug deal gone bad. This unfortunate trio tried to rip off the dealers and paid with their lives. The way they died was probably to serve as a warning to others that might entertain the same idea. I have sent

DNA to be compared with the DNA you have on file from the Arizona murders, but Matt and Harry are sure we will have a match."

Everything is moving so fast. Jake tried to put it all in perspective. "Matt has seen these pictures? Who is this Harry person? Is Matt here? And McNeil knows about all this?" Jake looked to Cara, who had the same questioning expression on her face.

"Matt is here, but we know there are many eyes watching, and if it is Sandro, it is too risky and too dangerous for him to chance being recognized by coming here today. Harry? Well, Harry was Matt's commanding officer in Kuwait and is now the chief of homicide in L.A. County. He has seen firsthand what this butcher can do. He recognized his handiwork and called Matt, who called McNeil. Harry and I were asked to meet with McNeil and were briefed on the situation here and the task force you're working on. You, Dr. Biscayne, are the one person who would know even before the DNA results are back if this was done by this Sandro."

Jake looked at Han-Kiong. "You want me to examine the bodies?"

"Matt thought it would be a good idea, and so I would appreciate your help. I've seen some butchering in my days in L.A., but this..." Han-Kiong shrugged his shoulders.

Everything went dead still as both women tried to absorb what they had just heard.

Cara broke the silence. "I have left a message for my contact at the attorney general's office, and as soon as this weekend is over and the festival is done, Cipriano's involvement is over. If I could put a stop to the drugs ending up here right now, without endangering my family, believe me, I would. If the drugs are dropped this weekend, I want them out of here and off my property. This is too great a risk to my family, and I will not allow it to go on a minute longer than I have to."

Han-Kiong caught the look that passed between the two women. "Can't say I blame you. This is one bad-ass son of a cracker, but connected. Before you do anything, consider this: if his drugs are taken, and he knows who you are and wants revenge, your family might be in more danger than if we use the drugs to nail this guy."

Before Jake had the chance to read what was going on behind Cara's cold brown eyes, Cara turned toward the door. "We have guests arriving in a few hours for dinner. If you will excuse me, I want to check on my family."

As Jake watched Cara walk out of the room, she felt the pangs of her abandoned heart. Cara was leaving her again to go to Maggie and her children. Her family.

CHAPTER TWENTY-THREE

"**W**hat the hell did she say, Rachel? She's pulling the plug on this operation?"

Josh McNeil yelled into the telephone, his face puffed and red with anger. "No way is that going to happen. We're this close, Rachel, this close. We now have him placed here in the States and connected to the murders and drugs in L.A. This bastard Sandro is our guy and the head bastard in Mexico for the Rivera cartel. If we can nail his ass and he gives us names and places, we can shut the pipeline down all the way to Colombia. Do what you have to do, but get her and this situation the fuck under control! She's not going to bail out on this now, Rachel, we're too close."

McNeil slammed the telephone down and paced around his office, thinking, then went back to his desk and sat down. *Why have I not heard from you, Jake? What's going on with you and Vittore?* McNeil picked the telephone up and dialed Harry Sweeney's number. *If there is one person that can help us bust this guy, it's Matt Peyson.*

Sweeney, Matt, and Han-Kiong sat at a table toward the back of the smoky bar. Sweeney raised his glass to the bartender for another Jack Daniel's, while Matt nursed a tequila and Han-Kiong drank his usual, black coffee with four sugars.

"That stuff will eat your liver out, Harry."

"Yeah, I know, Hank, you've been telling me that for years now."

"How'd she take it when you showed her the pictures, Hank? Did she seem all right?"

Han-Kiong looked at the bloodshot eyes of the clean-cut border patrol agent. "Biscayne? Hard to say, Matt, neither said much to me or to each other. I had no doubt she thought the killings were done by this Sandro. It shook them both, but the vineyard owner turned ice on me and said if the drugs were dropped, she wanted them off her property ASAP. Then she just walked out."

He finished his coffee and picked up his briefcase. "I need some sleep, and from the looks of you, Matt, you could use some too. My wife complains that I spend more time with dead people and Harry than I do her. And she's right. Don't drink all night, Harry. Matt, Biscayne is going to take a look at the bodies in the morning. Early. She asked if you would meet her there. She said she'd call your cell phone when she left Cipriano."

Harry watched his friend exit the bar, but he was thinking about Matt's relationship with Jacquelyn Biscayne. The beautiful blonde studying to be a doctor was all the young captain had ever talked about when they were fighting in the Persian Gulf War. *Matt planned on asking her to marry him when he got home. I wonder what happened.*

"How's your mother doing with all this, Matt? Has to be hard on her knowing what Sandro has done."

Matt finished his drink, then stared into the bottom of the empty glass. "She loved him as her own son, Harry, as much as she loved me. I always thought he was her favorite. He could always charm his way around her, around everyone. She hasn't said much, but you can see the hurt and shame in her eyes. She blames herself, as if it's her fault, like she did something wrong raising him. She watches the door half expecting him to come through it with that bigger-than-life smile on his face making everything all right. He was a brother to me. Just too hard to figure, Harry. I would have bet my life on Sandro—and did. You know Craig and Sandro saved my life in Kuwait. The two of them stayed with me when my leg was shot full of holes and we were separated from our unit. They were almost out of ammo by the time the rescue helicopter arrived."

Harry emptied his glass and motioned for another. "You want another, Matt?"

"No, I'm good."

"I might be butting my nose into your business, Matt, but what happened between you and the lady doctor? I figured you two would be married and have a passel of kids by now."

Matt's blue eyes deepened with a faraway look. "Yeah, me too, Harry. It just wasn't in the cards for Jake and me, I guess."

"She's made quite a reputation for herself as a profiler with the Bureau and as a forensic expert. I know Hank is pretty familiar with her work and has read many of her papers. I thought it was strange, her working undercover on this task force. When did she start working in the field?"

"We haven't seen much of her for over a year now. She's been pushing herself, taking one field assignment after another."

"Sounds like the lady is running away from something."

"Jake has been running most of her life. First to please her dad because she wasn't the son he wanted. Then to be the best to make him proud of her—and now to find his killer."

Harry looked at Matt questioningly as Matt continued, "Jack Biscayne had come out of retirement and was working as a consultant on a case involving the flow of drugs from Mexico into Nogales. He had come across something and had called me to meet him in town at the café, that he had something to tell me. He never showed. I found him sitting at his desk, slumped over with a garrote hung around his neck. I always wondered how someone could have gotten that close behind him in his own house to kill him. It was Sandro; Jack had connected him and wanted to tell me first before he turned the evidence in. Sandro told Jake all this that day at his ranch when he escaped."

"She ever get married, Matt?"

Harry wondered if he had hit a sore spot when Matt didn't answer right away, and when he did, his voice had hardened.

"She fell in love, Harry, probably for the first time in her life, but the person walked out on her, just disappeared."

Harry's cell phone rang. "Damn, there goes the feel of a pillow under my head tonight. Sweeney here."

CHAPTER TWENTY-FOUR

Cara's heart pounded erratically against her chest as she held baby Stephen to her breast. Her every instinct was that of a mother to protect her young. The word *Sandro* kept repeating in her head. She cursed whoever brought this threat, this evil into Cipriano and their lives. A million thoughts were running through her mind. The drugs belonged to Sandro, and one of her brothers was involved.

Reason, Cara, reason! Think! Does he already know who you are? No. If he did, the last shipment of drugs the task force followed would never have arrived. He couldn't know. Turning the drugs in if they show up now is out. There might be a chance of catching him by using the drugs, but my family has to be safe first. Cara knew what she had to do, and Rachel Slade could arrange it.

"Rachel, only you, I, and your most trusted agents are to know where they are until this is over. Agreed?...Good. My brothers will not even know where they are. They will be safe in Italy with family; the cartel cannot reach them there. Can you have the arrangements made by tomorrow?...Good. I will explain it to them in the morning, but tonight they will enjoy the festivities. Once they are safe, Rachel, I will do anything it takes to stop Sandro." *This time he is mine.*

Cara sat for a very long time watching Stephen discover the mobile hanging over his crib. She smiled with pride, then with adoration, as he clumsily reached up with the tiny fingers of his left hand and swatted at one of the colorful pieces.

149

"Hey, little man, are you going to be a leftie like your mom?"
Her index finger traced the silky-soft hair, around the shape of his
ear, then his toes. At the thought of being separated from her son,
a profound sadness from the depth of her being broke her heart. *I
love you, Stephen, and I promise it won't be for long. Maggie will
take good care of you until I come to get you.* "You be a good boy
until I do, you hear me?"

Maggie's voice came from the doorway. "What have you
promised him now, Mom? A pony or his own Disneyland?"

Maggie was startled to see the anguish and obvious distress
on Cara's face as she turned to Maggie and held her hand out.
Frantically, Maggie crossed the room to Cara's side. "What is it?
Is Stephen all right?"

Cara searched the face of her beautiful, loyal friend. "I need
your help, Maggie. It's time I told you about Stephen. And Jake."

Maggie felt the pain of every word as Cara told her about
Mexico and why she'd ended up in Italy. It was difficult to hear
the details of what her friend had gone through and that she had
been alone when Stephen was born. Maggie's heart stopped when
Cara told her the first results of the HIV testing were positive, then
she sobbed with relief when Cara added that the second one had
been negative.

When Cara stopped talking, they held each other, allowing
the tears to fall. As Cara pushed the strands of hair from Maggie's
puffy face, Maggie said, "You said you needed my help, honey.
What is it?"

"Maggie, there's more, and it isn't good "

"Okay." Maggie held both of Cara's hands. "Tell me."

Maggie paced back and forth in front of Cara. "Paulo is many
things, but involved with drugs? It's hard to believe. What
happens if—Oh my God, Cara, we need to get the children and
Grandfather to a safe place until this is over."

"That is where I need your help, Maggie. You are the only
one I would trust to do what I am going to ask of you."

After Han-Kiong left, Jake had sat alone in Cara's office. Sandro's name hung in the air, hovering like a death sentence. She remembered the day she had removed the dead fetus from the mutilated body of one of the girls Sandro had raped and murdered. She trembled, still hearing his words reaching in, ripping her heart out of her chest when he'd told her he was the one who had killed her father. Now she was to witness more of his butchery because they had let him escape that day.

Jake pushed thoughts of Cara from her mind, not wanting to think about the closeness they had shared only minutes before. She needed to talk to McKenzie and ask her to leave in the morning. She needed to see Matt. Her objective was to finish this assignment and get Sandro. Cara's concern was her family, and Jake knew she was not part of that family or Cara's life.

When she'd called Josh McNeil, Jake had been informed of Cara's decision to remove her family the next day to a safe place in Italy. The possibility of Sandro being in the States to oversee what they assumed was a huge drug shipment and Cipriano being involved made it a critical time and impossible for her to ask to be replaced. She checked in with the command center and the surveillance van, then went to find McKenzie.

Once she found her, Jake walked with McKenzie along the stretch of beach below the guesthouse, both in deep thought. Jake explained to McKenzie without breaching the confidentiality of the operation that Maggie, Cara's grandfather, and the children would be leaving Cipriano the next day and that it was too dangerous for McKenzie to stay.

They were just passing by an outreach of rocks when McKenzie stopped and pulled Jake over to sit beside her. "I could stay and help if you would let me, Jake. I want to. All you have to do is say I can. Let me be with you."

McKenzie had felt a distance between them since arriving at Cipriano the previous night, and although they slept in the same bed, they hadn't made love. Jake had come in, late and exhausted, turned toward the opposite wall, and gone to sleep.

"When this is finished, I would like us to go away for a while—a vacation. I would love to take you to the Isle of Erin and show you why they say Ireland breathes with a thousand glorious shades of green and sky so blue and clear you can see forever. I have a country home, in Salthill overlooking Galway Bay. You'll love it, Jacquelyn, and I would love to have you there with me." McKenzie laced her fingers with Jake's, not pushing for an answer, but her green eyes held hope.

A single cloud passed across the sun, darkening the sky, and a breeze blew Jake's hair across her eyes. She had the strangest feeling of being watched. She looked down the beach to see a few of the festivalgoers walking and enjoying the sun and sand, but no one seemed to be paying any special attention to her or McKenzie. Jake felt the same odd sense of warning she had felt earlier and her eyes searched across the water to the many dots of vessels anchored along the skyline.

"I need to get back, Kenzie, to get ready for the guests arriving tonight. I want you to have a good time. You've been added to the guest list and will sit next to me at the main table." Jake genuinely cared for McKenzie and felt bad about avoiding her questions. "Kenzie, I promise we will talk after this assignment is over. Can you wait and be patient with me until then?"

McKenzie pulled Jake in and kissed her softly on the lips. "An old Irish saying is 'patience is a virtue and its own reward.' I would wait forever for you, Jake."

Then, trying to lighten the mood, she pulled Jake along the path back toward the vineyards. "Come on, I have a dress I bought to wear tonight especially to knock your eyes out, love."

When they reached the top of the hill, McKenzie followed the path to the guesthouse while Jake went to a small storage garage located at the back of the main house that had been covertly transformed into a command center. She wanted to go over procedure and security before the crowds started to meander in. With so many people milling around, maintaining security was not going to be an easy task.

McKenzie had left a note saying she was going up to the house and to meet her there when she could. Jake stood in front of the full-length mirror, looking over her tailored black silk tux. Her blonde hair hung loose to the top of her collar, and the ruffled light green silk blouse brought out the green and gold flecks in her hazel eyes. She lifted one lapel of the waist-length jacket to place a small transceiver under it, then put on a pair of black onyx earrings that housed a minute receiver. She pulled up one pant leg, strapping a small-caliber handgun to her specially crafted patent-leather boots.

"Can I get everyone to sound off, starting with you, Mike." When the last agent had checked in, Jake walked up the path to the main house. She could hear the music and laughter emanating from the house and the outdoor area set up for dancing under the big oak trees.

Lanterns lighted the walkways and the large oak trees surrounding the house. The lights in the trees cast a soft glow to the evening and appeared to dance to the rhythm of the music. The smell of food wafted through the air, and servers with trays of delights mingled among the guests. The dinner and wine auction for charity attracted many patrons, especially the very wealthy from Montecito and other areas of the country, and they came to impress by spending money and by making the best dressed list. The cars lining the driveway ranged from custom Hummers to Lamborghinis.

Jake stopped on the path, sidestepping into the shadows, and fingered her lapel. "Has anyone seen either Paolo or Giancarlo yet tonight? Both are there...still in the house? I want constant observation on them, and let me know if they make any calls or if anything seems out of the ordinary." *I will be so relieved when tonight is over and the family has left for Italy.*

Jake entered the house through the kitchen, as she always did, and stopped to pour a cup of coffee and to say hello to Hattie, who was busy supervising the additional kitchen help.

"Well, Miss Jacquelyn, aren't you a sight for sore eyes." Hattie had her own thoughts about the beautiful woman who Cara seemed to be at odds with all the time. She had never known Cara to show as much emotion as she did when she was around her new assistant. Hattie thought the constant bickering was the way both women covered feelings that ran much deeper than either would admit.

"Thank you, Hattie, everything smells so good. Can I help you with anything?"

"You can take these trays out to the garden if you're going that way."

Jake took a drink of her coffee and stole a small sandwich off a tray. "I would be glad to, Hattie. I was just going out to look for my guest."

Cara finished her call to her uncle in Italy, relieved that he had told her to leave it up to him to come up with a reason for the visit that would not alarm her grandfather. She placed a call to the pilot of Cipriano's private jet and was surprised to find out that Rachel had already filed a flight plan and replaced Cara's pilot with one of their own.

She went out to the balcony, wondering how her grandfather would react to the trip to Italy, but confident he was strong enough to make the trip, especially in the comfort of Cipriano's jet. She stood in the darkness looking out over the grounds. An unknowing person would never suspect what was happening beneath the surface, lurking beneath the excitement of the evening's festivities. She was about to go in and check on the baby before going downstairs to play hostess when she saw Jake standing off by herself.

Cara never could hold back the desire she felt for Jake every time she looked at her, and this time was no exception. Jake's blonde hair captured the moonlight, and her black silk tuxedo was elegant, accentuating her long legs and slender, lithe body. *Oh, Jake, how beautiful you look tonight. It seems all I ever to do is disappoint you, and today was no different. I never considered your feelings or emotional state after learning about Sandro. I just did my thing and walked out. The least I could have done was stay and talk to you.*

Cara turned away when she saw McKenzie, looking elegant and gorgeous and with eyes only for Jake, walk across the garden toward the blonde doctor.

Maggie had been sitting on the darkened balcony, sorting though everything that Cara had told her earlier in the afternoon about the drugs and the possibility that Paolo was involved. Her divorce was not final yet, and it had been a long time, if ever, since she had any feelings for Paolo. Still, it was hard for her to believe.

Her father would be at the charity dinner tonight, and he knew she was divorcing Paolo. The only words he'd spoken, after she told him about the divorce, were to ask if Paolo had ever raised a hand to her or his granddaughter. She never could lie to him, and when she didn't answer, his face had darkened and all he'd said then was "Come home." He'd left away on business the day after she broke the news to him, and neither had broached the topic since that day. Had he known for sure the answer to his question, that Paolo had indeed raised his hand to her, and more, she had no doubt in her mind that Armanno Santini would kill Paolo.

Maggie sat in the dark, unseen, her heart aching as she watched the expression on Cara's face and the longing in her eyes as she looked across the garden toward Jake. There was no doubt in her mind, it was love. Cara loved Jake.

Her heart was heavy and the festivities didn't seem so important as she finished dressing and went to knock on Cara's door to see if she was ready to go downstairs.

"Come in, Maggie."

Maggie chuckled as she entered the room. "How do you always know when it's me at the door?"

Cara ran her hand down her abdomen, smoothing down her dress, and turned to look at Maggie. "I'm physic. Besides..." Her voice trailed off as she stared.

Maggie's hair was pulled back into a twist, with a single strand of soft curls on either side of her face. She was wearing a blue dress and a sapphire necklace and earrings that darkened her blue eyes and brought out her Mediterranean coloring. She was exquisite, flawless, like fine porcelain.

"You look stunning, Maggie! I forget sometimes that you're all grown up. How beautiful you are."

Maggie twirled around. "So do I meet with your approval?"

Cara smiled and held out her arm. "I will be the envy of everyone in the room."

CHAPTER TWENTY-FIVE

Paolo was occupied at the bar getting drunk, and Giancarlo was mingling with the guests. A distinguished-looking man in his late fifties, his thick black hair streaked with gray, sat with Sebastian Cipriano.

"You condone this divorce, my friend?"

"I am ashamed to say my son has not been a good husband or father to your daughter, Armanno. He has his problems, but make no mistake, I make no excuses for his behavior. We were wrong to think in the old way, having them marry without love. It has brought nothing but unhappiness to them both."

"It is hard to change the ways of our fathers, but I suppose we are not too ancient to try, my old friend." Armanno sipped his brandy. "Your granddaughter, Cara, has returned. This is good. I am happy for you. Speaking of granddaughters, where is—"

Tiana tore across the room, jumping into her grandfather's arms. "Grandpa, I missed you! What did you bring me?"

Armanno lifted Tiana up into his powerful arms. "What did I bring you? Do I not get a hug first, Tiana?"

Tiana squeezed her grandfather's neck. "Of course. I love you, Grandpa."

Jake was standing next to McKenzie, who was sitting at the busy bar, when the room took on a different buzz. The bartender mouthed a whistle and feigned a swoon as he playfully clutched his heart. Jake's eyes followed his and half the other eyes in the room toward the stairs. The bartender leaned over to McKenzie, who he'd been hitting on since she sat down, and whispered conspiratorially. "Gorgeous and hot, but untouchable. What a waste. Beauty, money, and both dykes."

McKenzie shot him a glare that could shrivel the best and opened her mouth to tell him that he had been hitting on a dyke all night when he moved to the other end of the bar.

Jake watched Cara, with Maggie on her arm, descend the stairway. The bartender was right about one thing: the two women were stunning. But Jake's eyes were only on Cara as she moved her long tanned legs down the stairs. The business suits and work clothes Cara usually dressed in didn't do the tall vintner/lawyer justice. She wore light makeup and a low-cut, backless white dress that clung to every curve, effortlessly sliding over silky olive skin. Her auburn hair hung loose to the top of her bare shoulders.

Jake felt a twinge, and her body tingled as she felt herself growing warm all over. She wanted to look away but found herself helplessly drawn to the woman she couldn't get out of her head. Jake held her breath, afraid to breathe. *Oh God! How can this be happening? How can my body still crave and want her touch beyond all, beyond everything she has done. Damn her, why does she have to look so...so...*

McKenzie remembered the woman who was with Cara in San Diego and was stunned. "That's little Maggie that Cara used to talk about! My God, I've never seen a more beautiful woman!"

Cara's thoughts had been on Jake since she had left Jake in her office with Han-Kiong. Her worried brown eyes searched until they connected with hazel ones across the room that burned into hers, making her legs tremble and her heart beat faster. She remembered the last time she'd seen that undisguised, raw emotion in Jake's eyes.

Jake had pleaded with her not to go and was so upset that they had words. They didn't have a chance to speak again before Cara had left Tucson for Mexico with Matt Peyson and Craig Ochoa. She had offered herself up as bait to trap a serial killer who was using the Arizona-Mexico border as his hunting ground. Little did they know it would turn out to be Sandro.

Cara hadn't been able to sleep, thinking about Jake and the possibility that she had lost her by going against her protests on such a dangerous mission. She lay awake in a sweltering hot, dingy hotel room above a cantina in Mexico, listening to the blaring sounds of tinny music and the smell of fried foods coming through the open window.

She was about to get up and chance the trip down the hall to the bathroom when she heard a noise at the door. Many women just disappeared without a trace or concern of the law in Mexico, and she knew to be cautious. Earlier she'd braced the back of the room's only rickety chair under the doorknob, but she knew with one good push the chair and door would give. Grateful that she had a handgun, she chambered a round, held her breath, and removed the chair, her hand on the doorknob.

When Jake fell through the door, Cara's heart was pounding out of her chest. The anger she felt toward Jake for taking such a chance with her own safety quickly melted under the look of desire and need in Jake's eyes as Jake pulled her down to the floor. They made more than passionate love that night in their relentless need to pleasure and give to each other. The moans and sounds of Jake's passion throughout that night would forever brand Cara's soul.

Jake's eyes followed every movement of Cara's body, focusing on the movement of her hips, the soft swell of her breasts. Cara's eyes locked onto Jake's. They needed to talk. She had to apologize for that afternoon, and she needed to keep her promise to tell Jake the whole story. As soon as they reached the bottom of the stairs, Cara excused herself and started toward Jake but hadn't gone far when dinner was announced, and McKenzie ushered Jake into the dining room before she could reach them. *After dinner, you and I are going to talk, Jake, and damn it, no one is going to interfere.*

Jake tried to avoid making eye contact with Cara during dinner. She knew she was being unreasonable, but it was annoying and frustrating to see the familiar way Maggie ran her fingers along Cara's arm and the casual brushes across her bare back as she leaned into her while they talked.

She struggled to maintain a cool façade, but the frustration was putting her on edge, and her tolerance was waning. Two conflicting voices were banging at her frontal lobe. One wanted to cause physical harm to Maggie or Cara, or at the least break Maggie's fingers. The other was the voice of reason, telling her she was on the job and that she was acting childishly, motivated by jealousy.

Her attention focused on Paolo, who was glaring at his wife and sister and getting more inebriated as the evening wore on. Giancarlo tried to get him to slow down on the whisky sours, but Paolo belligerently shook him off, spilling a drink all over himself. When he got up and left the table. Jake slipped away and followed him to a waiting silver-gray Mercedes sedan.

As she observed him, Jake noticed that Paolo's drunken gait miraculously improved as he approached the passenger side and got in. She talked into the night, watching the taillights fade into the darkness. "Run this plate, guys, California 3BBJ502, and put a tag team on him. We need to know where he is going, who he's with, and if he meets anyone. Everyone, stay on your toes and report anything that seems...odd." *Oh Lord, with this eclectic, how-to-live-like-a-millionaire bunch, anything could seem odd.*

Matt leaned back in the chair, his hat pulled down over his eyes and his boots propped up on an old crate, listening to Jake's voice echo low over the receiver. He rubbed his thumb over a two-day stubble of beard, thinking how good it was to hear her voice. It was a stabilizing force for Matt, giving him a sense of connection, of home. His mouth curled into a slow half-smile. *Better not let her know how much I miss her. I'll never hear the end of it.*

After the briefing earlier by Josh McNeil and with Operation Monsoon Rain on high alert, Matt wanted to be at the vineyard so that in the event that something went down, he would be there. He wanted to see for himself that Jake was all right, and he didn't want to wait until the next day.

Sandro might have cut her heart out, but Cara had ripped it to irreparable pieces. Jake was working to exhaustion and refused to feel, encapsulating her emotions and denying her pain. She ran from one assignment to another, always hoping to find a lead to Sandro. The intricate threads of destiny had brought her to Cipriano to face both her demons. Matt feared one could take her life, but the other, in its own way, was even more dangerous. Cara had taken her soul.

Jake was wound tight and felt the tension building as she walked along the path back to the house. She considered the fact that the car that picked Paolo up had been parked on a back service road so far away from the house. *Is Paolo our connection to Sandro, or could his behavior tonight be just coincidental?*

She stopped when she reached the garden, trying to push the impending headache off and the intruding thoughts of Cara out of her mind. She needed to think straight, and the images of olive skin and doe brown eyes were distracting and wouldn't go away.

"Are you all right?"

Startled, Jake swung around. She hadn't heard anyone come up behind her. Cara was standing there, the light of the full moon reflecting off her white dress and making it shimmer in the dark. Jake's heart stammered in her chest, her pulse quickening at the sight. For a moment, she was breathless. Then she remembered her resolve not to let Cara affect her.

Taking a step back, she defiantly locked eyes with Cara and attempted a tone of detached coldness. Still, her voice quivered. "Shouldn't you be inside with your guests?"

Cara took a step toward Jake. "I'm sorry about this afternoon. I shouldn't have walked out the way I did."

"Hey, I've been there before, remember? What do they say about the second time around...it gets easier? That's a lie. It hurts just as much. Damn you, Vittore, it never has stopped hurting!" Jake started to tremble as Cara took another slow step toward her, her eyes pleading, never breaking contact.

"We need to talk, Jake. I know this is not a good time, but when is? Every day since we've been apart I've wanted to tell you why I left."

161

Jake's emotions were near the breaking point as she pivoted around, putting her back to Cara in an attempt to get herself under control. "You can save your speech for the courtroom, Counselor. I'm not interested."

"I'm not going away, and we are going to talk." Jake could feel Cara's warm breath on her neck. It sent an instant jolt down her spine, making her knees go weak.

Cara's voice was low, almost a sob. "You told me the day you arrived here never to touch you again. But I am going to touch you, Jake, because I know you want me to touch you, and I need to touch you."

Cara closed the space between them and slid her arm around Jake's waist, pulling her possessively into her body. The air around them crackled with electricity, threatening a spark that would ignite them both. Her lips were a breath away from Jake's neck, her voice breathless and pained. "Tell me you don't want this, tell me you don't feel the same ache in your soul that aches in mine."

Cara moaned as Jake whimpered and pushed her body back into hers, one hand covering Cara's at her waist, the other sliding down Cara's thigh. The heat from Jake's fingers left a trail of scorching liquid fire along her flesh as they moved slowly across her thigh.

Jake's head fell back onto her shoulder, and Cara's lips found the pulse point on her neck at the same instant her hand glided up to cup her breast. Nothing else mattered. Jake could feel only Cara's touch and the tidal wave of emotions that surged from the depth of her soul. She turned in Cara's arms, running her fingers down bare skin to the smooth softness at the small of her back. Mouths met and tongues searched, equal in passion, equal in desire.

Jake pulled away abruptly, putting her hand up to her ear. "Matt?" *Oh God!*

"Sorry, Jake, you might want to have this conversation in private."

Jake stepped back, flipping over her lapel to show Cara the transceiver while trying to steady her breathing and willing her heart back to a normal rhythm. Cara nodded as Jake mouthed, "It's Matt," then turned shakily and hurried off.

Cara instantly missed the warmth of the connection. Jake aroused her and filled her with desire as no other woman could. Jake made the pieces fit and righted her world. She didn't want to live without her, not anymore.

CHAPTER TWENTY-SIX

Jake entered the darkened garage to see the lights from the monitors reflecting off Matt's face. She glanced at the two agents, relieved that neither indicated in any way they had heard anything that went on between Cara and her. Matt wore a smile from ear to ear. "You're a sight for sore eyes, lady."

Jake walked over and pulled Matt into a hug. "It's good to see you too, just not under these circumstances." Jake pointed to an area of the garage where a table and cot were set up. "Buy me a cup of coffee?"

Matt poured two cups of strong coffee and handed one to Jake, noticing the slight shaking of her hand. "McNeil thinks Sandro is on this side of the border and has a lot riding on this shipment. Major crackdowns of distribution houses in Phoenix, San Antonio, and Denver last week apparently have him sweating, and there are more to come. They're cutting the head off the serpent, Jake, closing off the pipeline. Word is, it all filters back to him and the Rivera drug cartel. They don't know what routes are under surveillance, and it's making them real nervous, maybe nervous enough to make a mistake. Seems our boys got a few million of Colombian money, too. The cartel is none too happy right now."

Matt's blue eyes turned to steel gray. "I saw those bodies, Jake. The girl was done the same way as the ones in the desert. It was Sandro, no doubt in my mind."

Matt's jaw clenched, and Jake knew what he was thinking. "It's not your fault, Matt, Sandro is not your fault."

"Hell it ain't, Jake, he stood next to me in Kuwait while I retched my guts out at the violation. He offended the laws of humanity, stood right there beside me assuring me the whole time that we'd catch the bastard responsible, and I didn't recognize it when it was staring me right in the face down in Nogales. Jesus fucking Christ, Jake, some of those girls cut up in the desert in Kuwait were barely in their teens! I should have stopped him there, and Mexico would have never happened."

Jake covered Matt's large hands with her own. Mexico had changed all their lives, and Jake's heart burned with the same desire for revenge. "We have a chance to stop him now, Matt, one way or the other."

Matt's face softened. Would he ever stop loving this woman? He didn't think so. But he was ready to go on with his life. "Hey, I talked to Kalani a spell ago, she said to tell you to get yourself home in one piece and that your Appaloosa foaled a beauty yesterday. Teresa named him Desert Star because he is the color of the desert and has a perfect white star on his forehead. She loves living on the ranch, Jake, she has room to run and ride."

Jake could see the light in Matt's eyes when he talked about his daughter. "Teresa knows you're her father?"

Matt's pride lit the garage. "Yep, Kalani and I told her together. She was okay with it, Jake. Teresa has been good for Maria, she and Teresa have been pretty close this past year. Kept Maria going, I suspect."

"It has to have been hard on Maria, Matt. Sandro was—"

"I know. She's opened the café every day for twenty-five years, and one morning when I went in for coffee, Juanita told me she'd called and said she wouldn't be in. I found her in his room sitting on the bed, just staring at all his trophies and stuff. She never said a word. Just got up and asked me to drive her in to the café. She never talked about him, never spoke his name for a year, and out of respect no one mentions his name when they are in the café."

Matt took both of Jake's hands in his. "Now tell me, what is going on with you and Cara?"

Jake's eyes shot up. "Nothing is going on. I know what you heard, but that was...well, that was..." Jake covered her face with her hands. "Oh, Matt, I don't know what is going. She just gets to me, I guess. That shouldn't have happened, she's...with someone else."

"Are you sure, Jake? Has she told you why she left Arizona?"

Jake searched Matt's face. "You know why she left, don't you. Can you tell me?"

Matt was torn. McNeil was very thorough and a stickler for detail and he needed to know about all the players. When Harry Sweeney's call brought Matt to California, McNeil had shared with him the details of his investigation into Cara's life, mostly for insight into Jake's likely reaction if she knew.

"It's not my place, Jake, that's up to her to tell you. You two need to talk about it. As far as her being with someone else, if you're talking about her sister-in-law, maybe you're right. But it's time you both put this behind you."

What aren't you telling me, Matt? Why did Cara leave? Maybe it is time I found out. With that thought, Jake got up and walked over to the two agents sitting in front of the monitors. "Anything on where Paolo is heading or who the car belongs to?"

"It's a rental. They just arrived at the Santa Barbara Yacht Club and are on their way out to a 145-foot Bugatti Silhouette registered to a Mariana Karos of Greece. It's been one big party on that boat for the last three days. We're running her through the databases now."

"Good, keep me informed and notify the Coast Guard not to let it out of the harbor if it tries to leave. And update McNeil if he doesn't already know."

Jake turned to Matt. "I need to get back to the house. I'll try to get back a bit later." She put her hand on his chest and smiled. "Will I be invited to a wedding soon?"

Matt blushed. "Could be, Jake. Yep, could be, if she'll have me."

"Oh, I don't think you have to worry about that, Matt." She kissed his check. "Gotta go. Later."

Cara sat with Maggie and her grandfather in the garden, watching Armanno Santini twirl his granddaughter around the dance floor. "Tiana sure is having a grand time with her grandfather, Maggie."

"Yes, but it is way past her bedtime." Maggie smiled, watching the delight in her daughter's eyes. "I guess it won't hurt for one night. Do you remember when you, Stephen, and me would sneak out—we weren't much older than Tiana—and climb those trees," Maggie pointed with her eyes, "during the festival to watch the dancing?"

Cara smiled, remembering. "Oh, yes! And the night Stephen broke his arm when he fell right on top of Mrs. Robinson making out with her driver. We were grounded for a month."

"Oh, God! I do remember that. It was so funny, we were laughing so hard and poor Stephen had a broken arm."

The song ended, and Armanno sat down beside Sebastian wiping his forehead with his handkerchief. "We aren't as young as we used to be, Sebastian. That one will wear us out."

Maggie leaned in toward Cara, squeezing her hand, and whispered, "Is everything all right? You seem a million miles away. Where is Paolo? Did he leave?"

"I don't know where Paolo is, Maggie, and I'm just tired tonight. In fact, I was just going to go upstairs to bed. I'll take Tiana up with me and tuck her in. You stay and enjoy, visit with your father a while."

Cara got up, gave Maggie and her father a good-night kiss on the cheek, and then went to fetch Tiana.

CHAPTER TWENTY-SEVEN

The figure sat in the dark, alone on the deck, blending in with the caliginous shadows that crept from bow to stern of the twin diesel–powered yacht. In the distance, a foghorn wailed a mournful warning that hung in the air like a portent of an impending storm. Ominous black eyes stared through the rolling mist toward the dim lights on the shoreline.

My beautiful Jacquelyn, did you think you could play this little game with me and win? You never could. Your weakness will defeat you again, and it will be my pleasure to teach you and your lover a lesson. This time one that you will not soon forget. So, C. V. Cipriano is actually the lawyer bitch, Cara Vittore. I knew our paths would cross again, Vittore. You and I have unfinished business.

Sandro had been incensed, beyond crazed, when he learned of the task force and how much they knew about the movement of his merchandise and his operation. The dead bodies were piling up as the cartel unleashed its terror and delivered its message to anyone suspected of giving information.

The high-priced whore delivered to the yacht the night before had earned her fee and more by taking the brunt of his anger and twisted mind. The classy, beautiful woman had been beaten, severely disfigured, raped, and dumped in a vacant lot and left for dead.

The door to the cabin opened, and a man walked out with a cell phone in his hand that he handed Sandro.

"*Sí*, no mistakes, my friend. We have a lot riding on this," Sandro said, then closed the cell phone. "How many knots will this boat do, Hector?"

Hector nervously thought, then blurted out, "They said it would outrun anything on the water, *Jefe*."

Sandro's lip curled in a twisted smile. He wouldn't need a whore that night. "We shall soon find out. Tonight I will throw a party of my own. And take care of some unfinished business."

"Did you have a good time tonight, Tiana?" Cara asked as she tucked the sleepy five-year-old under the covers.

"Uh-huh, Aunt Cara, thank you for letting me go."

"It wouldn't have been a party without you, sweetheart."

"Love...yo..." Tiana was fast asleep, dreaming of twirling around the dance floor with a knight in shining armor, as soon as her head sank into the pillow.

"Good night, baby, sweet dreams."

Cara changed into a robe and went into the nursery to get Stephen, relieving his nanny, Sorrin, to go downstairs to eat and enjoy the rest of the party. She settled in the rocker, listening to Stephen's contented sounds, humming to him softly as he suckled at her breast.

As she rocked, her mind replayed the scene with Jake in the garden. The past year had been emotional hell. Everything was a mess and not as it seemed, but she hadn't imagined how Jake had responded to her touch. That was real. Jake was one stubborn woman, but her body couldn't lie, nor could she hide the desire in her hazel eyes.

The corners of Cara's mouth turned in a tired smile as she looked down at Stephen, who was unwilling in his sleep to relinquish his mother's nipple. Cara was weary of the struggle and wanted her life back and her family safe and free from the ominous black cloud hanging over Cipriano.

Mixed emotions pulsated through Jake's body as she hurried along the path toward the house. She was determined to talk to Cara and deliberately kept to the shadows to avoid being seen.

Through the trees, she could see Maggie sitting in the garden with her father, listening to the music, and McKenzie engrossed in a conversation with Giancarlo and Sebastian Cipriano. She felt a pang of guilt about not spending more time with McKenzie, but she needed answers that only Cara could give her.

If she just wouldn't look at me the way she does with those sad brown eyes. It's like I am looking into her soul and can read her heart. I don't see the fire in her eyes that used to be there. Her eyes always reminded me of that electrifying anticipation brewing on the horizon before a monsoon storm—seething, ready to explode. What I see now is exposed, raw pain.

That thought triggered a memory of the time right after they had returned from Mexico just before Cara disappeared.

At first, they had clung together, grateful to be home and out of Mexico. But a few days later, unexpectedly, Cara had moved into the guestroom, telling Jake that she didn't want to keep her awake all night trying to get comfortable. Cara's wounds were painful, and Jake tried to understand. Still, down deep she was hurt and worried. Cara initially let Jake tend to her burns, but she had started tending to them herself while Jake was in town or at her office. Even when Cara's wounds began healing, she hadn't moved back into Jake's bedroom or touched her, other than a good-night peck on the forehead or cheek. Ironically, Jake hadn't been able to sleep a night since Cara left her bed.

Then, one night, she arrived home to find that Cara had prepared dinner, but Cara was quiet and only picked at her food. Jake, frustrated, tried to get Cara to tell her what was wrong, but she just said she had cabin fever and would be going back to work the following week. Then she excused herself, saying she was going to bed.

Jake sat alone at the table, at a loss for what to do. She debated whether to confront Cara and make her tell her what was bothering her or to allow Cara to tell her when she was ready. Later that night she was restless, lying awake, listening to the sound of a coyote howling off in the distance and thinking about Cara when the light from the guestroom shone across the courtyard into her room.

She crawled out of bed and went to the doorway. Cara stood naked in front of the floor mirror in her room, struggling to put ointment on one of the burns on her back. Jake felt hurt, wondering why Cara didn't ask her to help. She stood in her bare feet, watching until she couldn't stand it any longer, then stormed across the courtyard to Cara's room with every intention of telling her so.

When she came through the door, Cara didn't try to cover her nakedness; she just stood looking at Jake, her eyes filled with an undeniable hunger. By the time smoldering brown eyes reached smoky green ones, Jake's anger had turned to something else, and she was across the room taking Cara in her arms. She ached to hold her; she needed her emotionally and physically. Jake longed to touch and feel every inch of Cara's skin next to hers. In a hoarse whisper she pleaded, "Baby, I need you, please."

A strangled moan escaped deep from within Cara's throat as she picked Jake up and carried her to the bed. Trembling hands removed Jake's gown, and a worshiping tongue and mouth tried to exorcise the demon that lurked between them. Jake fell asleep at the dawn of a new day, thinking that as soon as she regained her strength she would return the gift she had just received from her beautiful lover.

When Jake woke a few hours later, Cara was gone. She hadn't seen her again for over a year—until the wine show in San Diego.

Hattie's day had been long and tiring, but the elderly woman persevered and was giving last-minute instructions to the kitchen help before she retired for the night when she spotted Jake slipping through the kitchen door.

"Miss Jacquelyn, would you mind taking this tray up to Cara? My legs aren't what they used to be."

Jake took the tray from her. "Not at all, Hattie, in fact I need to speak with her." Jake had seen blueprints of the entire house, but never having been any farther than the downstairs rooms, she had wondered how she was going to get upstairs without Hattie questioning her. *Well, that was easy!*

"Thank you, and my legs thank you, too. Turn right at the top of the stairs. Her rooms are all the way to the end of the hall."

Jake balanced the tray of tea and sandwiches as she walked down the hall across the cool marble tiles. This wing of the house was beautiful. The walls were adorned with frescoes in muted colors of sand and cream that depicted scenes of an old Italian vineyard and villa.

She stopped and put the tray down on a table outside an arched doorway. The door was ajar, and she was about to knock when she heard Cara's voice from inside the room, humming softly. She pushed the door open a bit more to see Cara sitting with her back slightly to her in a rocker. The room was dark, lighted mostly by the full moon and a small bedside lamp.

As Jake's eyes focused to the light, she could see that Cara was rocking Maggie's baby. Her head was bent toward the door as she sang, and Jake could see in her eyes her pure adoration and love for the child. Her need to know why Cara had left her didn't seem important anymore, and she stepped back to leave, inadvertently hitting the door with her foot. Startled, Cara look up to see Jake in the doorway.

"I—I was just...I wanted to..." Jake started to turn to leave. "It can wait until tomorrow. I don't want to wake the baby."

"Jake, please don't go. Come in."

Hesitantly Jake turned back toward Cara, not wanting to stay in the room. "Okay, for a minute. Oh, wait," she whispered, opening the door to retrieve the tray. "Hattie asked me to bring this up to you."

Cara swallowed, feeling as nervous and uncertain as Jake looked. "She has always wanted to fatten me up, and now I'm afraid she has made it her lot in life. Please, pour a cup of tea, then come and sit by me." Cara's anxious eyes followed Jake across the room, her voice barely above a whisper. "I want you to meet someone."

Jake's heart was hammering in her chest, and every instinct was telling her to bolt, to run. She couldn't sit and watch Cara holding her lover's child, but something in Cara's voice, the whole picture, held her feet like a magnet. An irrational fear gouged icy fingers into her stomach, making her light-headed.

She couldn't take her eyes from the scene and the baby as she watched Cara's fingers smooth across his cheek. It was taunting her, daring her mind to put it all together. She watched the scene playing out in front of her as if time had metamorphosed into a slow-motion version of itself, defying the laws of relativity. Cara opened the front of her robe and revealed Stephen latched onto her nipple with his little mouth.

An explosion of white light burst behind Jake's eyes, and she stumbled backward, her palms extended as if to push the sight away. Her subconscious was screaming, tearing at the walls, fighting to reveal a horrible truth.

CHAPTER TWENTY-EIGHT

"**Y**ou've just heard the deputy secretary of defense with the latest update on the search for the leader of a terrorist cell that is functioning in the United States. Sources report that arrests have been made in several cities and areas essential to our defense. It is also reported that documents obtained in the arrests indicate these areas have been targeted for terrorist activity. Stay tuned to this station for the latest updates."

Sandro clicked off the television, walked to the bar, and fixed a drink. He was staring at the shoreline when a voice interrupted his thoughts.

"*Señor*, a boat is approaching on the starboard side, running without lights."

Sandro's dark eyes widened and flashed a warning at the captain of the high performance go-fast boat, who was carrying two Uzi semiautomatics. Taking one of the guns, he stashed it behind the bar and barked, "Be ready."

Anger surged through every muscle of his lean body as he watched the figure climb aboard. "You fool, what are you doing here? You could have been followed!"

"I wasn't followed! Get this, Sandro, there is no way in hell I'm going along with this insanity. It isn't going to happen! I will get your cargo out of the country, but you need to be ready to leave this country tonight."

Sandro's eyes darted through the darkness, then narrowed menacingly on the man in front of him. He spoke, his voice slow and deliberate. "And how would you do that, my friend? Because of the high terrorist alert, everything is being watched. Nothing is moving out of this harbor or out to sea without a search. Anything that tries to cross the border, Mexican or Canadian, in either direction is under scrutiny. There is not an airport or airstrip, private or abandoned, that isn't under surveillance. If you had been more alert and careful, we would have known they were on to our little enterprise, and the venture with you, before this cargo arrived."

"The drugs are one thing, but not this, Sandro. I am warning you."

Sandro laughed through a mask of stone. His eyes grew as dark as the bowels of hell. "You are warning me?" The knife simply appeared in his hand. In the blink of an eye, he plunged it in below the man's xiphoid, ripping up and into his chest with such force that it tore through the sternum. Surprise froze on the dead man's face as blood gushed from his chest and foamed from his mouth.

"Get rid of this trash, but not in the water where it can be found. If they find a piece of the body, make sure it is a little piece that cannot be identified."

Cara kneeled beside Jake as she cried. "Can I hold you, Jake? Please let me hold you."

"Stephen is yours? Were you pregnant when you came to Nogales, when we were together? When you made love to me?"

Cara's blue eyes filled with tears. "No. Yes. I wasn't pregnant when we first made love. It was after...after we—I was pregnant the last night we spent together."

Jake's bewildered eyes searched Cara's face. "The last time—how? Who? Oh God! It was in Mexico, wasn't it! Sandro!" Sobbing, Jake put her face in her hands. "I wasn't there for you! I let him rape you!"

Cara held on to the sobbing doctor, telling her repeatedly that it wasn't her fault. Jake suddenly pulled away, lashing out from the all-consuming pain that was tearing at her heart, but still trying to be quiet so as not to wake the baby.

"How could you not tell me and just leave without saying anything! Did you think I wouldn't support your decision to keep the child? Damn you, Cara. Damn you all to hell! Did you doubt my love for you? Did you think Maggie would love your child more than I could?" Jake tried to get up, but Cara kept her arms around her and held her.

"You're going to listen to me, Jake, while I tell you the whole story."

Jake listened, first fear, then pain showing in her eyes as Cara spoke. With each detail, her body flinched as if the words physically struck her. Tears fell silently down her face as she thought how alone Cara must have felt during the difficult labor and premature birth.

"I came home because my grandfather needed me after his stroke. I did not come home to be with Maggie. I love Maggie, but we are not lovers. She has been my best friend for as long as I can remember. When I learned that my brother was abusive, I moved her into this wing, and she asked me to represent her in a divorce."

When Cara finished, both women sat on the floor in the still, silver light of night. Jake's voice was low and drained of emotion, but it echoed off the coldness in her heart.

"I don't know if I can forgive myself for allowing you to go to Mexico. I could have stopped you, but I didn't. And I don't know if I can forgive you for not trusting in me or in us." Jake stood up, feeling wearier than she could ever remember.

"Jake, please can't we just—"

"It's been a long night, we're both tired, and I need to check in."

She walked over to the sleeping baby lying in the middle of Cara's bed. In a voice tight with emotion, her eyes pooling with new tears, she said, "He is beautiful, Cara." She reached to touch the child, but before she could there was a knock on the door and the phone rang. Cara picked up the phone as Jake opened the door to find Matt standing there with McKenzie.

Matt, uncertain, shifted from one foot to the other as his worried blue eyes took in Jake's red, puffy ones. *She knows it all now. Maybe she can get on with her life.*

"I was worried about you when you didn't check in and both the receiver and transmitter went dead. I figured you were heading here to talk to Cara, but I wanted to be sure. I need to give you a quick update. There's been some arrests on the terrorism case, and as part of search for the group's leader, the 9/11 border protocols are in place."

Jake looked at McKenzie, who was listening to Cara on the phone. All three froze when they heard her terrifying words.

"You bastard, I will kill you! You will not be able to hide anywhere in this world if you hurt her. I will hunt you down and I will find you and you will die like the depraved animal you are. Make no mistake, I am rich and her father is richer and far more powerful than you could ever imagine in that mercenary little mind of yours. You should have done your homework before you touched her. She has nothing to do with this; it is between you and me."

The blood drained from Cara's face as she listened. Jake went to her side and started to say something, but Cara raised her hand to silence her.

"I will make the arrangements, call me back in one hour...No, this is a secure line. I am warning you, do not touch her." Cara hung up, her body visibly shaking, her eyes burning with hatred.

"Please wait downstairs and do not to do or say anything about what you just heard without my clearance before I can tell you more." Before anyone could say a word, she rushed across the hall to Tiana's room.

Jake glanced quickly at Matt and McKenzie. "I'm going to go and talk to her. Don't do anything until we find out what is going on."

She found Cara kneeling at Tiana's bedside, looking at the child who was sleeping soundly. Cara got up, brushed the tears from her eyes, and motioned toward the door. She asked Jake to wait in her room, then went straight to her office, closed the door, and dialed the number.

"Armanno, Maggie has been taken. I need your help."

"Oh God! Please, Cara, don't ask me to do this. I know what's at stake, but I cannot keep this quiet. And even if I could, Matt would never go along with it. I can't let you risk your life again. Please don't ask me to do this. I won't." Jake was frantically pacing back and forth. "Let us handle this, please, Cara. We can shut down the entire state and coast of California. We will find her."

"For the love of God, Jake, I won't take that chance with her life! If she isn't dead already, he will kill her. You know it, Jake; you know how he works. The only hope is to exchange me for Maggie. He wants out of the country and with the help of Maggie's father, I can convince him I can get him out. But he has to agree to let Maggie go first."

"Damn it, Cara, then what? He just lets you go?" Jake wanted to describe in detail the horrible wounds on the bodies of the women she had autopsied, all inflicted before they died.

Cara continued to throw on her clothes. "I believe in the law, Jake, you know that. I have tried to do this by the way of the law. Now he has Maggie. It changes everything. It has to be done our way now, Jake. All of your agents are being pulled off my property as we speak. Within minutes, Santini's people will be here to provide protection for my family and to sweep for surveillance devices of any kind."

She turned to see Sorrin, who had just entered the bedroom still putting on her robe. "Take Stephen. Under no circumstance are you to let him or Tiana out of your sight, even for a moment. There will be people with you at all times."

Sorrin nodded, picked up Stephen, and hurried across to Tiana's room, on the way passing two people dressed in dark pants and shirts who stood in the hallway outside Tiana's door. Two more stood at each end of the hallway.

Cara walked out on the veranda for a moment to see several guards along the expanse of the porch that wrapped around the upper rooms. A parade of cars and vans was exiting the vineyard, while several others were coming in with no lights on.

Jake was stunned. All hell was breaking loose, everything was happing too fast, and she had no control over any of it. "Cara, please! Just listen to me for a minute. They will never let you take Sandro out of the country. There has to be another way."

Cara strapped on her watch, glancing at the time as she did. "I have less than forty-five minutes before he calls, and I need to be ready. I've made arrangements to have you escorted to a safe place and guarded until this is over."

Jake straightened her shoulders, and with renewed strength, she walked up to Cara and stood nose to nose, her eyes flashing an angry, deep green. "You've made arrangements? I am not leaving. You will have to have me bound and dragged out of here, and that will waste a lot of precious time." Her eyes narrowed. "Trust me."

Cara fumed looking into the unrelenting eyes she had run up against before—and lost.

"Get this straight, Counselor. Where you go, I go."

Cara opened her mouth to protest when one of the guards appeared in the doorway.

"Excuse me. Mr. Santini is downstairs, Ms. Cipriano."

Cara hurried downstairs with Jake on her heels to see the distinguished-looking Armanno Santini run his hand through his thick gray hair as he sat at Cara's desk talking quietly on his cell phone. His brown eyes darted to Cara, then to Jake. "*Ringraziar l'Indossa Bastone, sarò per sempre nel suo debito.*"

Armanno hung up and spoke to Cara. "*Chi è questo?*"

"*È l'agente incaricato dell'investigazione,* Jacquelyn Biscayne." Armanno raised his dark eyebrows and Cara added, "*Sta bene, possiamo parlare davanti a lei.*"

Intense brown eyes searched Jake's face. "Cara tells me I can talk in front of you. What I say here will go no further."

"*Sì, capisco e no farà non.*"

"You speak Italian?"

"Yes sir, and many other languages."

Santini nodded, conveying the seriousness of her commitment with his eyes as one of his men waved a wand up and down Jake's body. When he held out his hand, Jake reached into her pocket, pulled out the small transmitter, and placed it in Santini's open hand.

"Thank you, Ms. Biscayne. Now, for your own safety, I will require your weapon."

Jake hesitated a moment, then reached down to remove the small handgun from her boot. She watched as Santini slipped it into his jacket pocket.

"Please, both of you, sit down. This Sandro, I have located him. He is anchored off the coast, this side of Wilson Rock and the Channel Islands. The boat is a fifty-foot fiberglass, invisible on radar, and was designed for top speed. Nothing can touch it. It is too risky to try to take him on the water or by air. It's equipped with state-of-the-art sonar and radar that isn't even on the market yet."

Armanno looked at the clock above the mantle of the fireplace. "When he calls, tell him he will be flown out of the country in my private jet and that it is being arranged and you need an hour to prepare. Assure him my plane is not being watched and that you have already filed a flight plan. We need to get him and his guest off the boat if we stand any chance of finding Magdalene. My sources cannot confirm she is actually with him on the boat."

Blonde brows shot up. "Guest?"

Armanno pinned Jake with a glacial stare. "What I have already told you prevents you from leaving or contacting anyone until this is over. Make no mistake; I would cut the heart out of this man myself and feed it to the vultures, and I have no use for the scum he is smuggling out of this country. But he has my daughter, and I will do what is necessary to ensure her safety."

Jake and Cara waited motionless for Santini to continue. Jake's mind was running through every possibility. *Sandro didn't just come here to watch over a drug shipment. Who could be so important that Sandro would risk exposure by taking Magdalene Santini to get someone else out of the country? Someone so notorious they wouldn't make it out because of the search for—oh God, no! The terrorist!*

Armanno could see realization dawning across Jake's face. "You know, and you are right, Ms. Biscayne. It is a game with the highest of stakes of all, the life of not only my daughter but of so many more. This Sandro must not know that we are aware he will be bringing another passenger."

Jake's body tensed, every muscle tightened as she jumped up out of the chair. Her training and instincts were to fight her way out of the room. Her eyes darted to the doorway, then to the double door behind the desk where Santini was sitting. She needed to get out of there. If she didn't, and they let this terrorist escape, she could be responsible for the murder of many innocent people.

Jake could see two guards on the outside door behind Santini and knew she wouldn't make it through that way. She swung around, ready to try for the doorway to the hall, only to see two more guards standing just inside of the door.

Everything happened in the matter of seconds as Santini watched the two guards approach Jake.

"I am sorry, Ms. Biscayne. I would not respect you if you had not tried."

CHAPTER TWENTY-NINE

Cara paced back and forth across the room like a caged
lioness, stopping nervously to stand over an unconscious
Jake, who lay in the center of her bed.

Armanno Santini set down the file he was reading. "I assure
you, Cara, she will be fine. She is just sleeping, hopefully until this
is over. I have been reading the dossier on your Jacquelyn
Biscayne. She has had quite an impressive career with the Bureau
as a criminologist and forensic profiler."

He looked across the room at the knocked-out-cold blonde.
"It is best this way. She could not have compromised who she is
and willingly accepted what we must do."

Cara nodded. Santini was right. Jake would risk her own life
and career but not willingly, nor consciously, the lives of others.

Santini studied the grown-up, beautiful woman his friend's
daughter had become. Tall and svelte, he observed, yet a
restrained strength touched those shoulders. She was the kind of
woman who turned heads, whose mere presence demanded
attention. He could understand why any man or woman would
want her, including his daughter. He had been aware of Maggie's
love for Cara in their youth, but dismissed it as the emotion of
adolescence. The look he had seen in his daughter's eyes that
night, however, was the conscious desire of a grown woman.

"You had an affair with her?"

Cara turned to face Santini, looking him directly in the eye. "Not an affair. I fell in love with her and I think she loved me too."

"What happened? Why are you not together?"

Cara's eyes darted toward Jake and she could taste the bitter words. "Mexico happened."

The piercing shrill of a ringing phone screamed through the room like a banshee. Santini sucked in a breath and Cara swallowed the acerbic taste of fear that coated her mouth, knowing this performance was the most important one of her life. Her hands steadied as her face took on the persona of the cool, calm, intimidating attorney who seldom lost a case. She picked up the phone, answering with one word.

"Vittore."

Sandro ran his finger down the side of Maggie's face and along the tops of her breasts. "You are quieter than your lover was. She put up a good fight. I never did get to break her as much as I wanted to. Now you, it would be such a waste for us not to enjoy what time we have left, don't you think?"

Sandro pulled the duct tape from Maggie's mouth. She sucked in a deep breath. She was afraid, but her eyes did not betray that as she calmly stared into the black eyes of the devil. "Touch me and my father will not rest until you are quartered and your filthy carcass hung for the scavengers to pick."

Sandro's laugh of amusement sent shivers down Maggie's spine. She started to shake as she saw the handsome face transform into a maniacal manifestation of pure evil. He pressed the knife in his hand between her legs, his eyes the bottomless black pits of hell.

"I spoke too soon. You do have the quick tongue your lover has." He spoke slowly as he cut up the front of Maggie's dress. "Tell me, is she man enough to satisfy a beautiful woman like you? Does she fuck you both at the same time, or do you wait your turn?"

The depraved pleasure on Sandro's face glinted off the knife as it cut through Maggie's bra. "Do you object to sharing her with

Jake? Matt did. I will never know why he just didn't gut her and take what belonged to him."

He ran the knife over the naked, flawless skin of Maggie's shaking body. She struggled and screamed, trying to buck him off, but he pressed the knife to her throat, drawing blood. And then he reached down to unzip his pants. "As much as it excites me to hear your screams, they might travel over the water, and we don't want company right now, do we? If you scream again, I will cut your tongue out."

He bit Maggie's nipple hard, drawing blood as he cut her hands loose. "I much prefer to feel your lovely hands on me, so I will be fair." Maggie clawed at his eyes, raking her fingernails down his face even as his weight held her down. An accented voice from the doorway caused Sandro to jump.

"I hate to interrupt your stupidity, but I do not think it wise to continue what you are doing."

Sandro removed himself from Maggie and stood unfazed, zipping up his pants to face a tall man with dark skin and black hair.

My god, I've seen him before! He's one of the pilots that works for Cipriano and my father. Maggie cowered in fear and shame, trying to pull her torn dress across her body as Sandro circled around the man, his anger seething, ready to erupt.

"And why would that be, my friend?"

Showing no fear of Sandro, the man threw a paper at him, then walked over to a cabinet, pulled out a pair of jeans and a T-shirt, and handed them to Maggie. "Get dressed." He kept his eyes on Maggie, making her blood run cold, as she turned her back to put on the clothes he had given her.

Sandro looked shaken as he read what was on the paper, anger written all over his face. "Fuck them!"

The man diverted his attention from Maggie to Sandro, his eyes narrowing in warning. "You will leave her alone. She is our passage. Her father is a very powerful man, as you can see. If he sees that she has been harmed in any way, there will not be a hole deep enough for you to hide in, and your drug-running partners will not protect you from this man. She will not be exchanged. Both she and the Cipriano woman will accompany us to South America."

"The agreement was the flight to South America only if she was returned and Vittore took her place."

The black eyes of the terrorist reflecting off Sandro's were cold and calculating, belying neither emotion nor remorse for his chosen path. His evil was a match for Sandro's. The difference was that the terrorist was not motivated by greed or the pleasure of the flesh or the pain of others, but by hate and an archaic, ideological, political cause, making him even more dangerous.

"You were planning on releasing her? I think not. You play with people and enjoy your raping and killing too much. Everything changed when you took this woman." *You fool.* "Now you will abide by my orders. I understand the motives of the woman who has offered herself in exchange. She is willing to sacrifice her life to get this woman back. Taking them both will keep her in check. Once I reach my destination, I need very little time. You can do with them as you wish then. For now, do not make the wrong decision—you will not live long enough to regret it."

Tears ran down Maggie's face as she sank to the floor against the wall as far away from the two men as she could get. She was helpless to do anything to stop Cara. She knew she would never see her daughter again, but she did not want Cara to die with her.

The terrorist continued, "We have an hour before we go to the airstrip. There is no point in me going back ashore."

They will think she is the only one who can pilot the plane and that our destination is South America. By the time they realize otherwise, it will be done.

CHAPTER THIRTY

Matt watched the crimson taillights of the last task force vehicle getting smaller and smaller until they disappeared into the night. He cursed under his breath, regretting the decision to leave Jake behind, inside Cipriano, feeling that some mighty powerful strings were being pulled to get Josh McNeil to direct his entire task force to pull out after one phone call.

"I don't like the smell of this one damn bit!" Matt slammed the passenger door of Harry's car and paced across the roadway, squaring his stiff shoulders in the direction of the vineyard.

"They up and haul their asses out of here and there isn't a goddamned thing we can do to find out if Jake is staying of her own free will? No way in hell, Harry, would she turn off her transmitter without contacting us!" *I know you're in trouble, Jake. I can feel it.*

Harry Sweeney chewed on the stub of the unlit cigar in his mouth. "That's private property, Matt, we just can't go barging in there without a warrant. And there isn't a judge, especially in this county, who will issue one based on an overheard phone conversation."

"Fuck it, Harry, if she doesn't call pretty damn soon I'm going in after her, and I don't care who gets in the way or whose toes I step on. I did hear the conversation before we were asked to leave the property, and my guess is Vittore's sister-in-law was snatched. All hell was breaking loose, Harry, and her father Armanno Santini was the one giving the orders."

Matt took his hat off and ran his callused hand through his sandy hair, then rubbed his chin. "My gut is telling me that Sandro is involved with this, Harry, and that something bigger than a drug shipment is going down."

"Now, Matt, don't go flying off the handle here. You called me down here to help, and we will figure something out, but we're not going off half-cocked until we figure out a plan here. I've made a few calls, and you're right about one thing, it is bigger than a drug bust."

Harry stood next to Matt on the deserted road in his slippers, a pair of jeans, and a crumpled suit jacket he had thrown on over his T-shirt. He knew he was risking his job and pension going against orders to help Matt, but they had fought a war together and you didn't desert a buddy. *You always had good instincts, Matt. Only a handful of people in the government can order an entire task force with so many agencies involved to stand down, and most are involved with national security.*

Jake struggled to open her eyes and to turn her head toward the voice beyond the haze. She tried to focus on raising her chest to take a deep breath in an attempt to move the reviving oxygen through her body. The left side of her brain battled to reason, to take control, to remember.

She realized she was lying on a bed with a soft covering across her body and that the voice, Cara's, was throwing her a lifeline, preventing her from sinking back into a bog of blackness.

"I have written these letters, I would appreciate it if you would see that they are delivered if I..." She hesitated, her voice cracking with restrained emotion. "And this is my revised will. I want Jake to raise Stephen in Arizona, but he will have a home here at Cipriano, too. Either way, I know that he will be loved."

Armanno Santini nodded, his dark, tired eyes searching the face of the woman standing in front of him. He knew the odds of her returning were slim to none.

"If they turn over my daughter, as agreed, for you—and I doubt they will—we will take them as soon as she is clear. If not, and they decide to use you both as shields to reach the plane, you will have to get Maggie clear enough for the sharpshooters to take them out. The plane will not leave the ground with my daughter in it."

Armanno hesitated before he continued, contemplating what he was about to say. "Cara, you know if the plane does get in the air, it must not reach its destination." His eyes and the lines etched across his faced deepened. "Do you understand?"

Cara looked over at Stephen in the crib beside the bed where Jake lay, burning into her mind the picture of the two people she most loved. She wanted to scream no, that she didn't understand how God could allow someone so evil to touch and destroy so many lives or why her son would be left without his mother. She wanted to wake up from this nightmare in Jake's arms and to see her face every day for the rest of her life, and she wanted Maggie to be safe and sound asleep in her own bed.

She knew what he meant. Armanno would do everything in his power to rescue his daughter, but Sandro and the passenger he was smuggling out of the country could not be allowed to escape.

Armanno didn't need a verbal response, he could see his answer in the look of anguish in the eyes of his daughter's only chance.

"I will try to convince Sandro that to release Maggie is the only way the plane will be allowed to fly out of here. If he does, you have your opening. Take it. If I get in the air with them, you will do what is right."

Cara sealed the last of the envelopes and handed them to Santini. "Now if you don't mind, I would like to be alone for a while with my son."

Santini nodded and tucked the envelopes in his breast pocket, then exited the room to leave Cara to her good-byes.

She sat on the edge of the bed, pulling the crib and Stephen closer. Tears stung her eyes, and her mouth quivered in a small smile as she looked at her son.

"Hey there, little man, have I told you that I love you today and yesterday and will for all your tomorrows. Your mom has something very important to do, and if I don't get back, I want you to know how much I love you and that I will always be with you. See this beautiful lady here, Stephen? She will love you as much as I do and will always be here for you, to help you grow strong and to learn all the right things. She will take you to your first day of school, kiss your skinned knees, and dry your tears over your first broken heart. I will be there too. You won't see me, but you will feel me, standing next to both of you."

She felt the ache of loss as tears blurred her eyes for the memories she might never have. When a shaky hand covered her own, she turned to see tear-filled hazel eyes. "Jake. I thought you were still..."

Jake's voice was raspy from the drug she had been given, but she managed to get up on one elbow and focus enough to look Cara in the eye. "Do you remember the day I told you that you talked too much, Cara Vittore? Well, you do. Now, please come here, I need to hold you."

Cara's sob was a cry deep from within her soul as she pulled Jake into her arms. "I love you, Jake. I will never stop loving you."

Both cried tears of loss, of sorrow, and of anger. Neither wanted to let go of the other, both afraid it would be their last time together. Cara lay in Jake's arms feeling the connection and strength of two hearts threaded together, beating as one, as gentle hands circled her back trying to sooth the ache in her soul.

Her voice was so soft Jake could hardly hear it. "This will be over soon, but if something should hap—"

Jake put her fingers against Cara's lips, her voice husky with overwhelming emotion. "Please don't say that, and don't you even ask if I would love and care for Stephen. He is your son, and I already love him. He has your beautiful brown eyes, and I think I even saw that crooked, irresistible little smile you have when you're pleading a case in front of a jury. If you want me—and you darn well better, Vittore—we will raise him together to be a good man. And you and I, Counselor, will grow old together."

Cara shifted to look into hazel eyes that reflected the same love she felt in her heart. Her lips brushed softly against Jake's. "Bossy thing."

Tears welled up in Jake's eyes. "I don't want to lose you again. Please, I am begging you, don't do this. Let me handle this and allow me to call for help."

Cara's fingers slowly traced across the face of the woman she loved, their lips but a breath away. "Shh. I want to kiss you. May I?"

Jake pulled her face down, and Cara felt the softness, tasting her tears, kissing her eyes and the corners of her mouth, then the exquisite gentleness of Jake's tongue asking for entry. Her lips parted and the essence, the threads of life that had been severed, reconnected. The energy surged through her senses, lifting the veil of darkness from her soul as it reunited in communion with Jake's. As the kiss deepened, her stomach clenched; it was more than mere desire and passion for the flesh, it was the fervor of the soul. Their need for each other was stronger than their portentous destiny that moved closer with each tick of the second hand.

Cara lifted Stephen out of the crib, holding him against her breast, then stretched out her hand to take Jake's, pulling her closer. "I told you I wanted you to meet someone. This is my son Stephen." Cara kissed her son on the forehead, breathing in his scent, then put him in Jake's arms. They had come full circle and neither woman wanted the moment to end, but a light knock on the door brought reality home.

Armanno Santini was standing, patiently waiting. He looked at Cara, then to Jake and Stephen. "It is time to go."

"Have you located either one of my brothers yet?"

"We're still looking. I have explained what is happening to your grandfather. You could not keep this from him any longer, Cara."

"Yes, I know. Does he know about the drugs and the possibility of one of them being involved in all this?"

"Yes. He is stronger than you think. He is downstairs in the living room with the rest of the staff and McKenzie Quinn."

Cara looked at Jake, but spoke to Santini. "I will be with you in a moment." She took Jake into her arms, holding her tight, then kissed her. "Take care of my son until I come home."

CHAPTER THIRTY-ONE

The door was open to the study next to the living room, and Jake's heart tripped as she watched Cara buttoning up a blue chambray shirt over a lightweight Kevlar vest. Two military-looking people, a man and women, dressed in black fatigues and combat boots stood next to her. Jake immediately recognized the woman assisting Cara, even with her blackened face and the dark hat covering her hair.

The woman quickly lowered her head and averted her eyes, probably hoping Jake hadn't seen her face. They had been roommates at the academy and became fast friends and allies, helping each other struggle through the inherent harassment and prejudices held by many of the male agents. They had provided moral support to each other in their efforts to ignore the hazing by the gung-ho, predictable types that thought women did not belong in a man's world.

Jake was sure it was her. *Liberty? What the—? I gave the eulogy at your funeral. You were supposed to have been killed in Afghanistan. Rumor was, you were working with an elite, covert group that reported exclusively to the president. How can you...?*

I was right! Sandro is trying to get the bastard responsible for the increase in terrorist activities in this country out of the States! That's why Santini said the plane would never reach its destination!

Liberty and her counterpart finished briefing Cara and slipped out through the kitchen entrance as inconspicuously as they had entered to wait in the helicopter for Santini and Cara to fly to the marina.

Jake quickly looked around the room. Sebastian Cipriano was handling everything well, but the strain was showing, so Hattie took him to his room to get his medicine and to rest a while. Jake asked Sorrin to take Stephen upstairs and to stay with him and Tiana. Then she went to McKenzie, slipped her arm around her waist, kissed her on the mouth, and smiled as she whispered something in her ear. McKenzie kissed her back, nodded, and casually went over to pick up the empty carafe from the buffet table.

"I could use some coffee," she said, then headed toward the kitchen with one guard following her, leaving just one with Jake.

Jake stood up, announcing she was going to the ladies' room, and walked toward the hallway with the guard on her heels. She leaned against the door on the inside of the bathroom and said a prayer before she shoved the vanity table against the door. *This had better work. Matt, please, please be there!*

Picking up the vanity chair, she threw it hard toward the window. The shattering glass startled the waiting guard outside the door, who yelled, then started to kick against the door. Jake scrambled through the bathroom window at the same time McKenzie stuck her foot out in front of the running guard, sending him sprawling across the kitchen floor.

Jake's heart was pounding out of her chest as she ran as hard as she could into the darkness, toward the grapevines that ran alongside the road. She dove head first into the cover of the vines just as she heard the yelling behind her.

"She couldn't have gotten that far, fan out and search!"

Her lungs burned and they felt like they were about to burst as she ran between the rows of grapevines toward the arched stone entrance to Cipriano. A shout close behind her had her sprinting onto the road. There was no point now in taking a chance of losing her footing in the loose, soft dirt. She was in the middle of the road, within yards of the entrance, when someone yelled, "We got her!"

She was at an all-out dead run when she passed through the gate and was suddenly blinded by the bright lights of a car. She took a chance and hurtled into the arms of one of two shadowy figures standing in the beam of the headlights. She could hear the pumping action of a shotgun and a gruff voice saying, "I'm homicide detective Harry Sweeney, and I would advise you boys to just turn around and go back the way you came before this incident gets out of hand and the newshounds catch wind of it."

Matt stood beside Jake as she doubled over, gasping, trying to catch her breath after she lost the contents of her stomach all over his boots.

"Damn, Jake, I'm glad to see you too."

Matt held his .45 at his side and squared his shoulders toward the dark figures lined across the road. He could hear a voice that seemed to be in charge saying, "Two, sir...Yes, sir...A homicide detective."

The next thing they heard was a command. "Pull back."

Jake was standing with her hands on her sides, sucking in air as she tried to talk.

"Slow down, Jake," Matt handed her his handkerchief so that she could wipe her mouth while Harry retrieved a bottle of water from his SUV.

Breathlessly, Jake blurted out, "Matt, it's Sandro, he has Maggie and he is going to use Cara to get out of the country."

"Kinda figured it was something like that." Matt's desire to take personal vengeance was almost palpable. Still, he kept his cool.

"Is this going down tonight, Jake? We saw a chopper leaving a few minutes ago, just before your marathon race down the road, but we don't have any way of knowing where it was headed. Harry has been ordered not to interfere with anything going on here."

"I know where it is going, Matt, and I need your help to get to Cara before both Cara and Maggie die."

Matt looked at Harry, who shrugged his shoulders and reached for his radio. "Guess I can come up with some excuse to get us a chopper."

Matt holstered his .45. "Let's hear it, Jake."

Liberty adjusted the range finder on the Crusader night scope of the matte black rifle, focusing until the tall woman standing on the pier was in the center of the florescent green reticle. It was imperative that if the shot was taken it be dead accurate. She would follow orders; she always had, without question, without emotion. It had been a long time since anything had shaken her, but seeing Jake earlier that night had. She wasn't sure, but she thought Jake had recognized her. If anyone could, it would be Jake, with whom she'd had a trusted friendship that had lasted until Liberty's untimely "death" in Afghanistan.

Liberty was the first woman recruited to be one of the covert and elite "President's Men." Having no family to speak of, she had only ever felt close to one person—Jake—and wished she could have told Jake her death was staged, but it was obviously against the rules. Liberty had chosen to give up her identity and become an invisible operative for the president of the United States. She couldn't remember when her heart had turned to stone, or when pulling the trigger stopped bothering her as she pulled the trigge, an intrinsic autonomic survival mechanism from one too many faces in her dreams.

In Liberty's ear was the low murmur of brief, coded messages only she and her team would understand, and those were on a need-to-know basis. Seeing Jake had been a surprise, and Liberty didn't know why Jake was at the vineyard or what involvement or role she played in the current scenario. But she did know the look that Cara had in her eyes when she looked at Jake, and there was no mistaking the one in Jake's as she looked back.

Liberty wondered what would have been if she had told Jake how she felt about her, then mentally corrected her thinking. *Now is not the time to reminisce.*

With her shirt sleeve, she wiped the sweat that was forming on her brow, careful not to remove the black from her face. She reached into her thigh pocket and pulled out a headband, then took her cap off and slipped the band on. She never used to sweat. Only nervous people sweat, and in her profession it was dangerous to be nervous. Not only could it distort vision, causing a missed shot, but a nervous person could hesitate—and that could be lethal, to the wrong person. Her record of kills was exemplary, one hundred percent accurate. She extended her hand, spreading her fingers. Not a hint of a tremor. She waited for a disembodied voice in her ear to tell her the targets were approaching the kill zone.

Cara stood on the pier, the gentle breeze coming off the ocean billowing her slacks and long-sleeved shirt. It was a warm night, but she felt goose bumps along her arms and a bone-deep chill that stiffened her knees and fingers. Her heart was pounding so hard it echoed in her ears as she watched the lights of the approaching boat. *Please, God, let her be on that boat and all right!*

It seemed like an eternity waiting, not knowing, for the boat to get closer. The minute transmitter sewn into the collar of her shirt allowed Santini and the assault team to hear her, but she couldn't hear them—wearing an earpiece would have been too easy to spot. The motors of the power boat cut back as it edged alongside the pier. Two darkly clothed figures in ski masks jumped off, mooring the boat to the dock.

Cara dropped her eyes and checked her mark. This was where they wanted her, where they would have the best shot. She was desperate to get closer as three people appeared on the boat deck. One of them stepped off and walked toward her. Her heart slammed into her throat as she recognized the chiseled features and black eyes of Sandro.

"Ah, Cara Vittore, we meet again. You're looking even more beautiful than the last time I saw you."

His stench of evil permeated her nostrils, nauseating her. "Where's Maggie? I need to see Maggie."

"Another beautiful woman, your lover." Sandro ran his finger down the scratches on his face with a sardonic laugh, his dark eyes taunting. "She is more of a fighter than you were."

Cara felt the fear choking her as blind rage lifted her hands, wrapping them around Sandro's throat. The adrenaline tightening her fingers wanted revenge, wanted to end the life of this abhorrence, this freak of mankind. "Where is she, you bastard?"

Sandro was on his knees, his face a lurid pallor, his eyes fixed on Cara's, mocking her from the bottomless pits of hell.

Armanno Santini could only watch helplessly from his vantage point as Sandro's hand slid along his boot, then the moonlight illuminated the flash of his knife as it repeatedly slashed into Cara's body.

A hand on Santini's arm restrained him from rushing to her aid. As much as he wanted to do something to save Cara, he realized that such a move could cost his daughter Magdalene her life.

Liberty waited, making no move as the team leader continued to speak very calmly and quietly in her ear. She focused on the target, her finger resting easy on the trigger, showing no emotion as she watched the beautiful woman stagger from the impact of the knife. She was ready.

"Can you confirm the objective?"

"Affirmative."

"Objective clear?"

"Affirmative."

"It's a go."

Maggie watched in horror as a dark stain spread along Cara's clothing and Sandro moved to grab her from behind, pressing the knife against her throat. Three muffled shots rang out. The two figures on the dock dropped instantly as Maggie felt a buzz and a brush of air along her ear. The terrorist standing behind her released his grip violently as he was knocked hard back against the boat railing.

Two forms in wet suits rose out of the water and into the boat before the man hit the deck. She felt the tape rip from her face and something being pushed into her mouth just before she was pulled over the side into the black water.

Liberty had a clear shot at her last target but hesitated. The knife was cutting into Cara's flesh, at her carotid artery. One slip and it would be over. Liberty waited for a directive, but none came. She had just begun to squeeze the trigger when she saw a figure she recognized running along the pier. It was Jake, and she was heading straight toward her target, putting herself directly in the center of Liberty's scope.

Damn it, Jake, I have the shot. What the hell are you doing?

Jake stopped running when she was within a few yards of Sandro and called out to him. "Sandy, it's Jake. Sandy, can you hear me?" She edged a little closer, hoping that something in Sandro's demented mind would respond to the name that she had always called him when they were children.

Sandro's eyes glazed over as he raised his head and looked quizzically at Jake.

"Sandy, Matt is here with me and we want to help you. Will you let us help you?"

Liberty kept her eye pressed to the scope and her finger on the trigger. The disembodied voice spoke in her ear. "Ghost, do you have a shot?"

Sandro's head was in her scope, just inches above Jake's shoulder. She could take the shot, but it could cost the life of the woman Liberty knew Jake was trying to save. It was as if Jake knew she held the woman's life in her hands as she looked purposely into the blackness, toward where Liberty was posed with her finger on the trigger. Her pleading eyes reached Liberty through the darkness.

"That's a negative."

The team leader had his finger pressed to his ear as he spoke to Santini. "Your daughter is safe and the target has been neutralized."

A look of profound relief crossed Santini's face. "Please give the woman a chance to save Cara."

"Ghost, proceed at your discretion."

Jake could see that Cara was bleeding badly and was barely conscious. If she didn't get help fast, she would bleed out. Her voice shook and her legs felt like rubber as she tried to edge closer. "Talk to me, please, Sandy."

"Jake?" Sandro's voice sounded bewildered, oddly childlike, but he kept the knife pressed to Cara's throat, tightening his hold. "Mateo? He is here?"

Matt stepped from the shadows and slowly moved toward Sandro. "I'm here, *hermano pequeño*. I need you to do something for me. Do you remember when you, me, and Jake were still wet behind the ears and we found that old knife in the barn? We decided to become blood brothers, *hermanos de sangre*, Sandro, remember? We vowed if one of us ever needed help, the others would be there? I need your help now, brother. I need you to let the woman go. The killing must stop, *mi hermano*."

Jake kept her eyes glued to the blood pooling on the wooden boards of the pier. Her mind was screaming, *There's too much blood!* Cara was limp, lifeless now, in Sandro's arms, and Jake couldn't see her breathing.

Sandro never said anything, but Matt could see the look in his eyes. He remembered that look, a little brother who used to trail after him like his shadow. Sandro's eyes cleared, and he smiled as he let go of Cara and reached for the gun in his belt.

"Adiós, mi amigo."

Matt felt Liberty's bullet whiz by him just before it hit Sandro between the eyes. As the blood of the man he had vowed to hunt and kill stained the ground at his boots, Matt wished he were home with the desert under his boots, warming the coldness that gripped his soul. He longed to see the faces of his family and hear the sounds of life awakening in the Arizona desert. He took his jacket off and knelt beside Sandro, covering his face.

"It's over now, little brother. I'm taking you home."

CHAPTER THIRTY-TWO

Jake sat with her bare feet on the front porch railing, savoring her first cup of coffee of the morning as the dawn of a new day announced itself over the Santa Rita Mountains. Whenever she could, she made it a point to allow herself the luxury of watching the breathtaking event, heralded by the spectacular colors on the Arizona horizon. The rain the night before had infused the air with the intoxicating, sweet natural smell of the desert as it thirstily drank in the life-giving moisture. She marveled at the trill of nature as the earth came alive under the spreading fingers of the sun, their magical touch warming and painting the desert with brilliant color.

She had arrived home the night before, and it felt good to be back in Arizona after being gone for months on an assignment out of the country. The ranch seemed empty as she sipped her coffee, waiting for Matt and Kalani to pick her up. They were married now, and Matt wanted to show her the house he had built for Kalani and Teresa on a piece of property out at the vineyard. Jake had sold her half of the vineyards to Matt, and he had taken on a new partner. The vineyard was prospering under the hand of the partnership, and it was rapidly gaining a name for its fine quality and variety of wines. She had to laugh when Matt told her the new owner could "feel the pulse of the grape." Seemed like he was learning a whole new lingo.

She had been on the move, in remote places, never staying in one place long enough for mail to catch up. She did get the one letter from Matt saying he and Kalani had gotten married and that McKenzie had moved to Santa Barbara, California, and was seeing someone, and that it was serious.

Distancing herself physically and emotionally was the only way Jake could survive the pain. Remembering Cara lying in a pool of her own blood, not breathing, still made her shiver. She would never forget the ear-splitting sound of the ambulance screaming through the night or the images of the trauma team working to get her heart beating when she coded as Jake stood by, helplessly watching. The days that had followed were a blur. Cara struggling to survive, comatose and on a ventilator. All of it seemed so unreal now as Jake remembered sitting vigil by Cara's bedside holding her hand.

She must have dozed and found herself jerking awake when she felt another presence in the room. It was Maggie, sitting quietly on the other side of the bed. Jake winced, seeing the swelling and bruising on Maggie's face where Sandro had beaten her.

Maggie didn't try to hide the love she felt for Cara. Jake could feel it. It was evident in her worried, blackened eyes. "Do you mind if I wait with you, Jake?"

They both loved the woman who lay between them, fighting for her life. Having both of them praying for her couldn't hurt. Jake's eyes filled with tears as she reached across the bed for Maggie's hand. "She can use all the prayers we can muster."

Days later, Cara was taken off the ventilator. She was breathing on her own and her EEG showed increased brain activity, but she hadn't come out of the coma.

Jake and Maggie had been taking turns going to Cipriano to check on Sebastian and the children. That morning, Jake had looked in on Stephen and Tiana, then gone to Sebastian's room to find the old man sleeping and Giancarlo sitting in a chair by the window. The usually composed, impeccably dressed man looked as if he hadn't slept or changed his clothes in days.

He had come forward after Maggie was kidnapped and Cara almost died, confessing that he had discovered Paolo skimming the books to pay gambling debts, but did not know about the drugs. Paolo was in way over his head and had drawn all he could from his trust. When Giancarlo had refused to lend him any more money, Paolo stole it from the winery and covered it by falsifying the books. Paolo was the one involved with the drugs, using the vineyards and the Cipriano jet to smuggle them into the country and illegally using immigrants as field workers. He raked off thousands of dollars, the difference between the salaries he reported and the substandard wages he actually paid. The body of Cipriano's pilot, Paolo's partner, might never have been found if his hastily weighted-down body hadn't surfaced offshore.

She turned to leave the room when Giancarlo's low voice called her back. "Thank you for being here for my grandfather and my family." Giancarlo looked at the face of his sleeping grandfather. "My brother has been arrested."

Jake simply nodded and went to her room to sleep a few hours, but she was restless, so she got up and went back to the hospital. As she walked down the dimly lit hallway of the ICU, the only sound she could hear was the continuous low drone of machines. She quietly pushed the door open to Cara's room, so as not to disturb Maggie if she were sleeping, only to find her in Cara's arms, kissing her.

Jake stayed long enough to hear Cara's raspy voice. "I love you, Maggie."

After she'd packed her clothes and made a few calls, Jake was on a government transport with the task force and Liberty Starr on her way out of the country to South America.

Satellite surveillance and the Monsoon Rain task force had amassed enough evidence for a roundup of many key figures in the Rivera drug cartel. The eyes of the world were upon them and on Colombia's connection to the reign of terrorism around the world, so it left the Colombian government little choice but to cooperate and show their good intentions.

Liberty was in charge of a unit directed into the Andean Highlands in Colombia, Bolivia, and Peru on a search-and-destroy mission of the coca fields. Jake had gone along as medical advisor and to render medical attention to the victimized natives held against their will and forced to work in the fields and to process the coca leaves.

A curious hummingbird, stopping to investigate the colorful liquid in the feeder that hung on the porch, caught Jake's attention and returned her from the past to the present and the beautiful morning.

She had slipped on her boots and was standing looking out toward the mountains when she heard the rattle of the truck coming down the road. She shielded her eyes against the sun with her hand and smiled as Matt's old work truck lumbered down the road.

Matt hopped out of the truck, throwing his hat on the front seat, and crushed Jake in a bear hug. "Damn it, Jake, it's good to see ya! You sure are a sight. Don't they have phones down there in South America?"

Jake laughed, looking over Matt's shoulder toward Kalani, who was getting out of the truck. The two women stood a few feet apart, and Jake could see that Kalani was about six months pregnant. Tears filled her eyes as she walked to her friend, rubbed her belly, and hugged her.

Kalani's arms went around her best friend. "Welcome home, Jake, we missed you."

The three friends had finished the tour of the new house and were sitting on the porch enjoying a nice breeze and a glass of iced tea. The house sat on a hill surrounded by a grove of cottonwood with a spectacular view of bluish purple mountains on all sides. It overlooked rows of new grapevines planted as far as the eye could see.

"It is so beautiful. I can't believe what you've done here. All the vines, and this house."

Matt and Kalani exchanged a quiet look.

"Hey, Jake, take a ride with me, I want to show you something."

Jake looked at Kalani, who smiled and held up her hands in protest. "Not me. I've bounced around in that old truck of his enough today."

The baby chose that moment to kick, and Kalani laughed. "See," she said, pointing to her stomach, "this one agrees. You two go on while I start dinner. Besides, I have a friend who is dropping off her toddler to spend the night."

Matt kissed his wife, and she squeezed his hand and whispered, "I'll see you later."

They drove for about fifteen minutes to a lush green valley that was Jake's favorite spot. Even as a young girl, when she wanted to be alone or to think, she would ride to that valley and sit on the hill under the trees and while away the day. She hadn't thought about it before, but that spot was part of what had been sold to Matt's new partner. Jake wished she hadn't come, especially when she saw the brand-new stucco ranch house sitting in the very spot that had always been just hers. Looking at the house, though, she found that she was impressed with the obvious time and love that was put into it. If she had built a home there, this would have been exactly what she would have wanted.

She looked at Matt quizzically when he drove straight up to the house. "I need to pick up something. It'll only take a minute and you might as well see the house and meet my new partner."

"I don't know, Matt, maybe I'll just wait in the truck."

Matt opened the passenger door and pulled Jake out. "Come on, Jake, I'll only be a minute."

Jake smiled and shook her head. "All right, but let's not stay long. I have a lot to do tomorrow, and I want to make it an early night."

Matt knocked on the front door. When there wasn't an answer, he opened the screen door and walked in.

"Matt, don't you think we should wait instead of barging in? It's getting dark, we should go."

"Kalani called to say we were coming. Why don't you wait in the living room while I see if I can round someone up?"

Before Jake could protest, Matt was out the front door, leaving Jake muttering under her breath, "How in the world does Kalani put up with him?"

She looked around. It was cozy, a fire was burning in the stone fireplace, and there was a familiar warmth about the spacious room. She walked around, touching the tables, wandering over to look at the bookshelves that lined an entire wall. The new owner had an eclectic collection of literature that ranged from Elizabeth Barrett Browning's sonnets to the latest child psychology books. One section held an interesting collection of law books.

As Jake ran her fingers over the rich leather bindings, she felt an odd prickling sensation down her spine. She pulled back her fingers as if they had been burned.

Somewhere in the back of her mind, she wondered what was keeping Matt, but a soft, melodic sound coming from the upstairs, and her curiosity, impelled her up the stairs.

As Jake stood posed to knock on the door that was slightly ajar, a feeling of the inextricable tangling of threads and coming face to face with her destiny washed over her. She pushed the door open into a room that felt completely familiar.

Candles and a crackling fire cast a soft, mellow glow across walls of earthen tones. There were floor-to-ceiling windows and doors faced to catch the sun, both rising and setting. The doors were open onto the deck, and the flames of the candles and the fire in the fireplace danced with the early evening breeze while shadows played across the stucco walls.

Jake's eyes were adjusting to the dim light when she felt another presence in the room. Her heart was pounding as she slowly turned to see a figure standing in the doorway, silhouetted by lanterns on the porch, making it hard to make out who it was. But her heart knew. She held her breath as the figure moved toward her, stopping within inches of touching her.

As a finger reached out to catch a tear that was threatening to fall from Jake's cheek, her head instinctively moved to feel more of the softness of the touch. She could smell the sweet essence, hear her own moan as her lips pressed against a palm, as she was pulled closer into an embrace.

"Welcome home, Jake."

"Wha...when...?" Jake felt Cara's lips press softly against her own.

"Has anyone ever told you that you talk too much, Doctor?"

The End

Other titles from
StarCrossed Productions, Inc.

Above All, Honor (Revised Edition)
Radclyffe
0-9724926-2-3 $17.50

Beyond the Break Water
Radclyffe
0-9724926-5-8 $19.50

Code Blue
KatLyn
0-9724926-0-7 $18.50

Fated Love
Radclyffe
1-932667-14-8 $18.99

Graceful Waters
Verda Foster & B L Miller
0-9740922-6-6 $18.50

I Already Know The Silence Of The Storm
Nancy M Hill
1-932667-13-x $17.50

Incommunicado
N m Hill & J P Mercer
0-9740922-5-8 $17.50

Justice in the Shadows
Radclyffe
1-932667-02-4 $18.99

Love and Honor
Radclyffe
0-9724926-4-X $17.99

Love's Masquerade
Radclyffe
1-932667-03-2 $17.99

Love's Melody Lost
Radclyffe
0-9724926-9-0 $17.50

Love's Tender Warrior's
Radclyffe
0-9724926-1-5 $16.99

Safe Harbor (Revised Edition)
Radclyffe
0-9724926-6-6 $17.50

shadowland
Radclyffe
1-932667-06-7 $17.50

Storm Surge
KatLyn
0-9740922-0-7 $17.50

The Price of Fame
Lynn Ames
1-932667-07-5 $17.99

These Dreams
Verda Foster
1-932667-04-0 $17.50

Threads Of Destiny
J P Mercer
1-932667-12-1 $17.50

Tomorrow's Promise
Radclyffe
0-9740922-1-5 $17.50

To find more great books by these authors and many more, visit our Web site at

www.starcrossedproductions.com